ARTERIAL

RED

GERALD BARLOW

ISBN 978-1-64492-688-8 (paperback)
ISBN 978-1-64492-689-5 (digital)

Christian Faith Publishing, Inc.
832 Park Avenue
Meadville, PA 16335
www.christianfaithpublishing.com

Printed in the United States of America

Excerpt from *Vinnie's Little Book of Colors*:

Arterial Red: An enamel (oil base) color; a semi-transparent crimson hue, usually used in gold leaf window work as a "fill." It is prized for its deep brilliance and long-lasting clarity.

Contents

1

Dove Logic

Sometimes, life just happens. We have a couple of fans out on the back-porch ceiling to stir up the flies in the lazy afternoons and I forgot to shut them off the previous night. My wife, Marti and I had been comfortably ensconced in the darkness talking, reviewing the day, holding hands and sipping iced apple tea. It was so nice that I simply forgot to switch the fans off when we slipped off to bed. Perhaps I had other things on my mind. We were almost asleep in the quiet when I picked out the gentle swish of the fans on the porch. I could have gotten up and shut them off, but the bed and Marti were warm. I snuggled in and drifted off.

A pair of doves had been trying to nest on the porch and shooing them away had become a breakfast ritual. I didn't think much more about it. Birds are smart enough to know when they're not wanted.

Our life on the edge of farm country brings its interesting challenges—no biggie. This morning, as I came out of the bath, there was a soft thud against the glass porch door, so I investigated. I just had to follow Scampers, the cat. He was doing the crazy dance, trying to get to the velvety form lying on the deck just beyond the glass. *Feline forensics?* Little swallowed mews accompanied his motions, sad and hilarious at the same time.

The still-warm body lay on the doormat, soft and gray brown and still, a bright drop of crimson on the breathing hole of its beak. The rising sun caught it with a wet sparkle. The bird had broken its neck trying to land on the slowly spinning fan blades. It would be like me trying to jump on the blades of an idling helicopter. I guess doves are not as smart as I would have thought. I gently disposed of the body (just to frustrate Scampers). He hadn't earned this one. I tried to show it a little dignity.

One would think that humans are smarter than the average dove. But perhaps not. Perhaps we are just as trapped by our emotions as the birds are in their instincts.

I should introduce myself. I'm Vincent DiMora, known to my friends as Vinnie and to most of my customers as Vinnie the Brush, a sign *painter*, part of a dying breed, the brothers of the brush. I, that is we, (my wife Marti lives with me). Well, sure. I've just botched this all up, haven't I? I'll begin again, my wife and I live in Riverglen, a small town smack in the middle of California's central valley. Marti works in the flower trade, and I have a small sign shop. Day to day, it can be an exciting life as I never know what I'm going to be asked to do.

2

Monday, Monday

Monday mornings could be a challenge, but despite my experience with the dove, I was looking forward to the week. I'd just stay clear of helicopters, right? I had a full slate of projects already ahead to work on at the shop, and I was mentally painting away as I drove to breakfast. I was multitasking, whistling even though I challenge you to identify the tune, and telling God he had done a good job constructing the beautiful day. The sunlight was peeling the dingy night from the brilliant treetops and with the cloudless blue sky above. I predicted it would be another California 10. I had no idea just how right I was. Silly me. I thought the scale went *up* to ten (in beauty) not *down* to a ten (in anxiety).

On Mondays, we review our choices and yearn for the chance to start over. It was deeply embedded in the metadata of the Creator's plan when He designed the week of seven days for humankind, and I have just lately figured it out. I don't have to scrub the disk, or reformat it, to begin again. I just get out of bed, and it happens automatically, fresh and new all around me.

Monday can be the best day of the week. It is the first day of the workweek for most people, and it is usually a clean slate *(sorry, white board)* wherever you look. There is the scent of adventure in the air, and the possibilities are endless. The future is constantly changing, and best of all, Monday is usually the easiest day in the week for a sign painter.

During the weekend, people often remember that sign they meant to order and when they get to work Monday, they see it's not up there and panic. So, the week begins, they rush into my shop, jump on the phone, or e-mail like I'm "911-sign." But even though the day becomes interruption-filled, I have the rest of the week to accomplish things in. Whatever I don't get done today I can do tomorrow, or the next day. No worries, right? There's little pressure. It's not at all like Friday; frightening Friday, the day when everything HAS to be finished. This is what usually fills my head while I'm driving to breakfast. This is the junk that usually accompanies my breakfast at Eddie's on Mondays.

But this morning, I wasn't caught up savoring the possibilities of work or the tantalizing thought of bacon. In fact, my mind wasn't even on work; I had a more pressing focus. It was almost Marti's birthday. *That* was the most important project this week, and the truth was that I still didn't have a clue what to get her.

Since the morning was beautiful, I decided to drive my '54 to work just for fun. I do my best thinking in my street rod. I'd been working off and on for the last three years on the 1954 Chevy Panel truck. I'd only been able to drive it in the last six months, and it was still a little rattily around the edges. I love it. I mean, smog laws notwithstanding, when you push the throttle, it goes; and when you hit the brakes, it stops. It's a hoot. Under that primered, fat old metal skin, it's really a '94 Chevy. LT-1 engine, TPI fuel injection and everything lie below the old truck patina. The only thing that gives it away is the ground-scraping stance and the big fat tires peeking out back. It's a Camaro in bib overalls.

When I finally get some more money, I'll get the interior done, insulate it, and stop the rattles. Marti won't mumble so much then. I have to admit that she's cooler about it than I expected. She says every boy needs a project, and then she grins at me. Hey, how come women are allowed to do that and men get criticized for it? What's PC? Isn't that condescending? I don't always know what to make of that look, but I guess overall, she approves. I figure it's a look of love because I know she doesn't see the truck like I do. She sees the grey primer and the rust spots, she hears all the rattles, and she laughs. To my eyes, it's already finished—painted, upholstered, and riding *smo-o-oth* down the road.

3

With Jelly

The sun was just beginning to work its way down the tops of the tall palm trees as I thumped down the road towards downtown. The palms are the first quirky thing most people notice about Riverglen—these sentinels lining the avenue. They seem out of place, a little Middle Eastern flair standing above the native trees. They stately guard the entranceway into town. Just a breath of valley breeze and the tops begin swaying to the CV rumba. Only fourteen trees, but out here in the flatlands, we grab what we can for landmarks. Everything else this morning was still in mellow lavender shades, and the sky was clear and pinkish-blue. The sun was now just cresting the Sierras. It was a perfect fall day and perfect painting weather for me.

Riverglen is geographically in the middle of the Central Valley of California. Still, it remains a small town struggling with growth and agricultural zoning issues. Everyone was only too happy to let Stockton have all the fame and the freeways. None of the folks really want too much expansion here; that's why most of us moved to the valley or came back home (to here). But growth brings economic health; so exactly when is it *too much*?

And that's the problem. Everybody has their own opinion, don't they? Breakfast at Eddie's is where they share them (the opinions), and it can be a real education if you open your ears while you eat. When you live in a small town, you learn all the local folklore. Eddie's has the best coffee in town excepting that new espresso place out by the college *(but it doesn't have any "history")*. I think the city folks call it cache. Eddie's is that; Eddie's is full of history.

The main highway used to go straight north through the middle of town, bisecting everything neatly into the haves and the wanna haves—the East side and the West side, the tracks in between. But since the sixties, the freeway had zoomed around the western side of the city limits, and some of the lines have gotten muddy. All of a sudden, commercial growth shifted toward the off-ramps. Easy access became the new priority.

Islands of strip malls anchored by name-brand stores hung like fruit from the busy ribbon of black. Now it wasn't so clear where the city was and where it was not. The neighboring farmland became broken up and chipped and endangered. The downtown was shrinking, people with foresight having moved out to the new malls while others held on to a dream of renewal downtown. The charm of the old buildings on Main Street was worth only so much. Unfortunately for us, many of our Main Street buildings are inherited by relatives in the Bay Area as the old owners die off. These inheritors have other concerns; they are people who just collect the rent. Many of these buildings have been allowed to decline without the always-needed maintenance, and once the roofs go to pot, well, not a unique story.

"Try Riverglen first" is an incantation repeated by the locals, and they're right. Buy it downtown or in town, and the city will flourish with economic health. It was in the paper and on bus benches all over town (some of which I had lettered), but it was like trying to raise a body from the grave. The town might have well been named Lazarus. The downtown needed divine help, and God seemed to have other priorities at the moment.

Eddie's is on the old highway, now renamed Riverglen Boulevard. I had rolled the windows down so I could hear the exhaust echoing back off the storefronts. Just a block from Main Street, the restaurant still has the power to collect most of the businessmen each morning. Breakfast at Eddie's has become the biggest unofficial service club around. I pulled the '54 into the lot, being careful to hit the entrance diagonally. When you drive a lowered car, you learn all about driveways. I cruised until I found an open slot near the back. I saw the space next to a new white Chevy ex-cab pickup. I climbed out and looked the pickup over as I chirruped my alarm button (You bet I have an alarm!). There might be a new Chevy to pinstripe in my future.

The front of Eddie's building is straight '50s—stainless ribs and quilted facets. Eddie and later, his son Eddie Jr., could never bring themselves to update it, and that's good because now vintage was back "in retro style" again. People coming through town often stop to get their photo-op out in front. It's like a time warp.

I stepped around the newspaper racks that someone had jostled out of line and pushed the big glass door open. I had lettered the name in platinum and gold leaf years ago. The red fills behind the letters were still bright and warm, catching the morning light as I swung it open. They looked like strawberry jelly. That job had been worth several months of breakfasts.

Coming into Eddie's is a very sensual experience; the smell is as unique as the metal fascia outside. Flapjacks, bacon, coffee, eggs, applesauce, you name it—these are all part of a unique sensory experience. Steamy enticing smells and the soft roar of voices envelope you upon entrance.

I headed for a place at the counter where I usually sat. Megs (Megan, my favorite waitress) waved at me and dropped a cup and saucer at my place, returning in a second to fill it.

"How ya doing, Vinnie? Ain't it nice weather today?"

I told her the sky looked good and sampled the coffee. Megs was a good waitress—warm, friendly, and shallow. She didn't want a conversation, she wasn't looking for a relationship, she wanted you happy. Happy people are good tippers.

"You busy today, Vince?" the suit to my left asked. I say "suit" because there weren't many at the counter at this hour. Most of these early guys were chambray-and-jeans types: contractors, farmers, truck drivers.

Most of our local suits don't get going until eight o'clock or so; the bankers and real estate guys come in with the Stockton Bee or the Wall Street Journal and eat in a booth by themselves with the paper spread out. Everyone here now had a ball cap on advertising some trucking outfit that hauled cattle feed or offered artificial insemination. Hey, it's a dairy town!

Clareson Tribble (the suit) was different from the yuppie stereotypes we see in the downtown area. Clareson liked to talk, and he had an eye for the local sports and such. He had the ability to carry on a conversation with anyone without looking bored, and I liked that. He could step down to almost anyone. I'm far too opinioned for that, but I had to admire the ability in someone else. Clare was Mr. Flexibility and that made for a successful realtor.

"Not too bad, Clare. I have work to do, but nothing real pressing."

"I thought I might get your opinion on the Marchant Building on Main...?"

"Yeah?"

"We have a buyer who wants to develop it into small professional offices. They are going to polish up the marble floor and make the entrance very posh. There will be a central receptionist with a desk in the foyer. They're working it out with their architect and the city. Have several lessors lined up—investments, a medical billing service, a new lawyer, maybe a paralegal too. They need some kind of ballpark figure to set in their budget for the entrance sign and the directory inside."

"That sounds interesting, Clare."

"Could you meet me there, oh, say eight thirty-ish? I have a meeting with them at ten, and it would help me out to have some kind of figure. I won't hold you to it."

Why do they always say that? "Sure. Be glad to. Eight thirty." He went back to his toast and coffee, and Megs looked down the counter at me with her eyebrows raised. I nodded, and she sallied up with her pad at the ready.

"Short stack and a small piece of ham?" She nodded at my words and flitted away. The conversations at the counter were mostly about the local high school football team. Since coach Birsen retired, the team just hasn't had the same fire. That new quarterback, the Sorenson kid, is pretty good, but not as consistent as he might be and so on. I heard three conversations going on at the same time, and they were all essentially the same. Practically everyone had seen the Friday night game. Everyone had their own read on the action and the appropriate solutions. As I watched the game, I was glad I wasn't the new coach. Football was a serious town event.

When Marti and I moved here in the '60s, we joined a local church and held craft sales in our garage just like all the locals, but it never seemed to "take" like it should. I've never figured it out. Maybe if we had been born here, it would be different.

Marti has her friends from work at the flower shop, and I have my regular customers like Clareson, but we don't really have many close friends. We count them on two fingers, well, maybe three. The first reason is easy; we're not Swedish. Not that Swedes are bad; I'm not prejudiced against them or anything (at least I don't think I am). It just seems like they all know someone in Minnesota or they are related by second cousins, or something. I'm Italian, but since my parents passed on, it hasn't meant that much to me. I figure I'm an American and that's enough. But it never seems to quite do it in Riverglen society.

I guess I was listening to the conversations so closely that the "clank" of the plate of flapjacks startled me. Megs smiled, "Caught you sleepin', Vinnie?"

"Yeah, guess you did. Thanks for the cakes. Got jelly?" I'm a sucker for jelly on my hotcakes.

"Sure," she said, and she popped up a jar of "mixed fruit" from under the counter. Hotcakes, flapjacks, griddle cakes, Eddie's had them down pat. I thought about the work waiting for me at the shop this week as I savored each bite.

As the only sign painter in the local area, my workload changes daily and is as varied as you could imagine. I had friends who could specialize in hand lettering or automotive pinstriping since they lived in a large city, like Sacramento or Fresno. I envied them. Although, I suppose doing the same thing every day might get to me after a while. Signs by Vinnie was never boring; that was sure. There was always something different to do. Riverglen always had some interesting project to offer me. I find myself doing signs half the time, and truck lettering and striping the other half.

The trade is funny, though. You could never count on it. Take the truck trade for instance. It wasn't always trucks. Busses, farm equipment, pull tractors, street rods, restorations, I get to do it all, just not as often as I would like. But praise the Lord, often enough to keep my fingers fairly sharp.

I left a couple of dollars under the too-soon-empty plate and went over to the register by the Reagan T-shirt pressed flat in its frame. In 1970, Ronnie and wife stopped here on their campaign tour down the valley. Eddie was so proud of it that he had T-shirts made that commemorated the fact. It gave everyone in town something to talk about for at least six months.

You know, now that I think about it, I don't think I've ever seen anyone in town actually wearing one of those shirts. (Now if he'd have let me design the shirt, *but that's sour "mixed fruit," isn't it?*)

4

Opening Up

The sun was up all the way when I left the restaurant parking lot. I headed down Main Street toward my shop on the west side. I rolled the side windows down again. I was "high school cool" for a few blocks of vacant glass fronts, the bright morning reflecting in their dark emptiness. Old time pictures of Main Street show thriving business traffic with parking always at a premium, even as late as 1980. That year, the all-knowing Cal Trans began building the freeway bypass around the town. *Well,* I thought, *change always brings things you don't expect.* It wasn't like anyone purposefully "did in" the downtown, and the new shopping centers are modern and convenient, I suppose. I caught myself buying things there sometimes. Life can be a confusing jumble of loyalties.

My shop was on the manufacturing side of town. Lots of big trucks go grumbling up and down my road, and a few stop at my shop for their lettering. Loads full of fruit and poultry products, spreading feathers and squashing dropped peaches or tomatoes on the roadway. Such is life.

I pulled into the side yard and shut the truck off. Someone was waiting for me at the front door, sitting in their sedan. I didn't recognize it. I try to get here ahead of people, but Monday morning always holds a surprise, like I said. People often got their ideas over the weekend and stopped in to see what they'd cost. Monday could be very good to me, but if they couldn't afford what they wanted, I was often just as disappointed as they were. The sign on the glass door said, "Signs by Vinnie" in gold leaf and etching. I was proud of that even if I never got any call for that kind of fancy work anymore; at least they could see what I was capable of.

I unlocked the back door, went through the shop, and opened the front door. "Mornin', Vinnie!" It was Delbert McCaughey, another local realtor, getting out of the beige Taurus.

I should mention at this point that there are two kinds of realtors: those who are in it for the money and those who have an actual personality. Del had a personality and a sense of humor. I really liked Del.

"Hey, Del. What's DelMac up to so early?" I palmed my keys and flipped on the lights as I went back in.

"I think I have a buyer for the Marchant building." Now I knew Del had the listing on the building, but when Clare had spoken to me, I figured he was representing the buyers, the other side, so I didn't say anything. It was none of my business. If I had asked, they would have both thought I was looking for an edge when all I was interested in was the lay of the land (and the job), so I kept quiet.

"Vinnie, the guy wants some ideas on a flashy directory in the entry, at the base of the stairs. He has several prospective tenants and wants to firm up their leases as soon as the building clears escrow, so we need a drawing to show them we are serious, and he's willing to pay for it."

I thought that was a nice touch, that he was willing to pay me for my work. Strange how even your friends see the sign business. "Sure, Del, you want to give me the specs?"

"Can you come over there around nine? I can get the office open and then meet you back there. You can see it for yourself."

"Sure, Del, but could we make it a little later? I have some stuff to do first. Maybe nine forty-five?"

"Ah, sure." He thought about it. "See you there, then."

I looked at the Felix the Clock on the far wall; it was 7:35 a.m. As I turned back, he waved as he closed the door of his Taurus. I turned on the shop lights in the studio and came back through, flipping on the computer and the radio. I filled the coffee maker and looked at the big magnetic board with the work orders lined up across the top. I try to set a schedule in my mind each Monday based on job priorities. I had two large signs to get done this week, and they both required coating out ("Coating out" is painting the background, in sign talk). If it's done right, the board will last ten to fifteen years; and if it's not done right, only a year or two. That's the difference in sign painters. I could start that first so that they would dry today. I could letter them Tuesday. There were the job-site signs for the roofer, six of them, but all red copy on white stock. Since those boards were pre-painted white, that one was easy, just cut the boards up and paint the edges. I heard the machine hiss the final spurt of coffee and thought about where I might have put my cup down on Friday afternoon.

Just as the cat's paws neared 8:30 a.m., I set a new message on the answering machine, grabbed my clipboard, and headed out the back door. I was just about to roll it shut it when a pounding began. I thought about it and then went back in, staring out at the front door from the darkness of the workroom. Someone was beating on the front door even though I had hung a "Back by 10:30" sign on it. Well, maybe it was important. I went back through the office and unlocked the door. It was a kid, his gray primered CRX parked diagonal across the handicap space in front.

"Hey, man, do Ju do stickers?"

"I don't know. What do you want?"

"Ju know, like on the windshield."

"How big do you want it? What is it going to say?"

"Hey, just up on top, you know. Just a couple of words, man."

"Can you tell me what the words are, or is it secret?" For me, it's a thin line between politeness and belligerence. He grinned a vacant smile at that. That look and the three-fourth cock-eyed hat position said it all. I was an "old guy," and a gringo at that.

"R-e-d-r-u-m, thas what I wan'. In red."

"In that, that Old English stuff, man?" I mimicked back at him.

"Yesss, yasss!" He shouted and jumped up and down as if I worked for Publisher's Clearinghouse. People seem to think I can read minds, but most of the time, it's obvious. It's just a question of looking around to see what the trends are. I knew what he wanted as soon as I saw the car. Our trends are usually about two years behind the big cities like San Jose and LA. Someone gets an idea, and as soon as they act, all their friends decide to do it too. Herd mentality.

"How big?" Now that I knew what he wanted, it seemed that I was trapped in this conversation. If I did it without this part, he would say it needed to be bigger or longer or a different color after I cut the letters, and then I would have to do it a second time. I had to get him to make the decisions. Doing fifty-dollar work for a twenty-five-dollar sale was not unusual, but not very profitable.

"I dunno. About this big?" He held his fingers apart.

I pulled out my pocket tape and handed it to him. "I like to use the marks and numbers on this. Go out and hold it up where you want it." He boogied back out to the car and tried several sizes. I guess he wasn't stupid, just fixed in the sloppy street-jargon that only described a few things well. I looked at the cat and saw it had been ten minutes. I hoped Clare wouldn't be too upset if I was a little late.

"About three and a half inches tall and thirty-eight inches long." He handed the tape back. I got his name and told him the price for the vinyl letters, and he said that was fine. "Ju gonna do it right now?"

"I can't, my man. I have an appointment. I'll have it ready by noon."

"Oh, man. I was hoping to get it, like, on before then." His beeper went off, and he flipped the little thing out of his pants pocket to read it. "I got to go." He said as if he had to use the facilities, dancing back and forth in place.

"I can't help you then. I have to be somewhere right now too. I can do it when I come back. That's the best I can do."

"Hey, well, hold up on it then. I'll be back in a while if I can't get it done sooner."

Swell. I locked the door again after him and ran out the back.

5

A Late Appointment

Main Street looked like a ghost town even at 8:30 a.m. I passed all of the empties and again thought about how life here had been twenty years ago. I guess I live in the past, in all the old photographs filled with the old businesses. When we moved here it was a big deal to come down the few evenings before Christmas, looking for the little gifts that fill in the cracks. The big ol' Woolworth's was booming then. That was one of my first gigs, to paint festive watercolor "splash" signs on the big front windows. You could spend an hour inside there and not even know it. Rows and rows of tables piled up with the little things that made life easier, interesting, and fun. Now you go in Walmart and get trampled in the narrow aisles by strange, tattooed folks, and everything for sale is plastic or worse. Where did all the metal go?

I parked in front, next to Clare's black Seville STS. The building's front door was open so I went in but didn't see anyone waiting. The foyer could be nice with the right trimming. It had the twenties marble square floor, still rich in color after years of hard use. The developer had marked out a wall to remove to allow room for the receptionist. There was a wide staircase leading to the second floor hallway. The lower hall led to the three or so offices on the ground floor. I remembered there had been a good barber working in the back suite by the alley door. You could see your friend's cars in the back parking lot and stop in after work. It had been almost like Eddie's, without the food.

I called out, but there was no answer, just the empty echo. I hate to prowl in someone else's place, but Del would be here soon, and then it might get real confusing. I went back down the dark hall, but I could see that all the doors were closed. The parking lot was vacant beyond the glass doors at the end. Something on the floor slid off with a clank as I kicked it, and I chased it down. It was a small ring with a few keys on it. I thought I had pocketed them when I got out of the truck. I'd better have Marti look at these pockets for tears. I went back to the stairs and began to climb. I never go upstairs except in tract houses. Marti likes to pretend we'll sell out and move into something newer, so we spend some Sundays looking in the new subdivisions, trying them on for size. Old staircases are so interesting. They have an ambiance in their sound and width. The creaks add to their character. The new ones sound like they aren't built right, like they're brittle somehow. You felt secure climbing the Marchant building. It had been built with space to spare. Tract houses had barely enough width to drag the vacuum along with you.

The hall was glistening up here; someone had varnished the wood floor. The side windows gave a view of the tarpaper roof next door and beyond it, the empty street. There were four doors off the hall. Each was painted deep maroon and displayed scars of past nameplates beneath the gloss. They were all closed, but there was artificial light peeping under the third. Since the sun was behind me, I figured it was electric, and I tried the knob. It was unlocked, and it opened. That was my mistake.

Clare had been on time and was still waiting for me. All I could see of him was the bottoms of his shoes and the crimson flood oozing over his Rotary Club jacket. He was lying face down in a growing puddle on the shiny wood floor. I stood there, so shocked I couldn't move. It was very quiet, and I realized that I was holding my breath and gasped for air, a mistake, as all the funky smells in the room rushed to fill my thoughts.

I looked around the room. CSI would note the details, not me. The air in the empty office had a wet fetid smell, and I almost gagged. Dust, floor wax, and the wet coppery scent that just couldn't combine with it; the blood was still very fresh. It seemed it felt far too normal to be observed, as I were in an I.R. game or a movie. One half of my brain was screaming in panic and the other half was calmly collecting details.

I heard a shout echo up from below. "Vinnie, you here?" It was Del, early of course. I backed out and closed the door (not touching the handle again), went down the stairs, clinging tightly to the banister, and we used his cell phone to call 911. Their response didn't take long. A shiny black and white slid into the curb and two of the younger "finest" jumped out and ran in through the front door.

One of the wonderful things you get with town growth is "new hire." Most of these young policemen graduated from the academy these days and looked for jobs in the smaller communities. Better chances of advancement, easier duty, and better surroundings to raise a family. Sound reasons, I guess. The downside was that we had a force with a large percentage of inexperienced men.

The older officer asked us to step outside once we clued him in to the situation, while his partner anxiously climbed the stairs, hand on his side arm. It looked to me as if he touched everything he could reach on the way up but, hey, I'm not a cop. What do I know?

It took a few minutes, and the officer came scrambling back down, yelling for his partner at the top of his lungs, the whites of his eyes betraying his experience (or inexperience). The front doors were propped open now, and his shouts echoed off the empty glass walls lining the street. With a noisy flutter, a flock of the downtown pigeons took off and began circling the building as if to help identify the source of the trouble.

6

Regrets and Tortas

I didn't get back to the shop until noon. I was still too anxious to think about eating, so I had a cold can o' tea and began coating those boards out on sawhorses in the back room. I had rolled the big door open, and the sun was warming up the inside of the room. As I watched the yellow glitter of the wet paint strokes, I thought over what I had told the police. It was so hard to feel the reality of Clare's death, when I had just watched him eat his toast. He was gone from my life, from everyone's lives.

I had answered the officers' questions as best as I could. Del had expressed a little anger at me afterwards that I would listen to both of the realtors, but I explained that I didn't know who was making the decisions and I wanted the job. It really didn't matter to me whose money I took. He finally said he understood, sucked back his anger, and went away; but I knew he was still fuming inside. I wondered what his vanity was so puffed up about. That's awful, isn't it? You can be convinced about the truth of some matter, but your "old man" keeps the emotional fires stoked inside long after the rationality has concluded. At least he will until you take the shovel away from him.

As I had driven to the shop, I wondered if Del understood that he could very well be a suspect in the murder. *Hey, I could too.* Who knew what motives the officers could imagine with the two realtors' competing interests? From the police's perspective, they were in contention for 3 percent of…*of what?* I thought about the building. Historical marble floors and stonewalls. Good location if someone ever breathed life into the downtown area. Who knows, if a good little restaurant comes in nearby and maybe a bookstore, the people will come back. It might be worth a couple mil. So Del might be anxious about $60,000. Even I could get nervous over $60,000.

It took me until two o'clock to calm down, and finally, my stomach decided I should hit one of the burrito trucks that park down by the Southern Pacific tracks that divide the downtown. I nodded at all the vatos who checked out my old truck when I parked. Their taste tended toward the gold-plated McLean wire wheels and those fancy accessories they stuck all over, but they appreciated the work I'd done so far. I did some pinstriping for them in town, now and again. It was easy to do the "old school" striping *chingaderos* they like; I was there forty years ago. Just because our tastes were different, I didn't see any reason to be impolite. Every boy needs a project.

I drove back with my *torta de jamon* (ham sandwich) steaming on the seat next to me. I pulled in by the big back door and went to open the little pass door in the big one, but the lock wouldn't work right. It took me a minute to realize I wasn't using my key ring at all but someone else's...*where had these come from?* I had my hands full of sandwich and bottled drink, and I finally dug out the right key and stuck it into the lock. Once the answering machine was turned off and the front door unlocked, I had time to think it out. I pulled out the key ring and realized it must be those keys I had kicked in the hall. I looked at them, only four hanging on a chrome split ring. They weren't mine after all. I should have given them to the investigating officers, I suppose. Then the phone rang, and I dropped them in the desk drawer as I picked up the phone.

Blessedly I didn't think about the murder again until I drove home. I know it sounds callous but somehow, the experience got packaged as unreal and filed under all the other Monday concerns. Then five o'clock came and business was put aside. Driving the hot rod didn't seem as much fun anymore as real life kept playing gruesome commercials in my head. I hardly noticed the traffic on the way home. I tried to focus on what to get Marti. Jewelry was an option, but I used it frequently for these occasions. She shopped at the country shops in town, so decorator stuff was probably out. I could check, though. I looked forward to sitting with her at the restaurant. Our daily debriefing was one of the high points of the day for me, and she'd agreed to meet there after work.

Twenty-six years of living together tends to build habits like early supper, talking through the day's battles, seeing if we won or lost, marking the scorecards for each other. I realized I had been repressing all my emotions about finding the body, and I thought about just how I would tell her. You know by now that I like to tell stories, but I wouldn't need to embellish this one. The facts were interesting enough, bare.

Finally, on the patio at La Bamba, the noise of happy conversations began to crowd out most of our cares. Luiz, our friend, took our orders, and we sat back watching the people and the evening bird migrations. We have a large population of magpies in town, a large black-blue-and-white bird about the size of a raven. Every evening, they seem to gather on the northeast side of town. It was like watching bomber formations fly over, each member wing to wing in the lavender sky, headed to their meeting. It was so regular an event that the other customers didn't notice it, yet it always fascinated Marti and I. The restaurant was only half-full on Mondays; Luiz's pretty cousin kept our chip and chopped cabbage and salsa bowls full. Marti had something on her mind. I could tell because she didn't ask her usual questions until the burritos arrived.

"Lina is pretty bored tonight," Marti commented as she chewed her first forkful.

"Yeah, she seems to watch the door a lot. I thought she was just anxious about the small house tonight, but I'm beginning to think she's expecting someone." We ate in silence, savoring the tangy goat cheese mixed in with the green tomatillo sauce. There must be over fifteen Mexican restaurants in town, but nobody makes green sauce like Luiz's mother. Her daughter Lina was serving as the patio hostess tonight. She had a nice, friendly, flirty manner that everybody loved. It was as much a trademark as the green sauce. The sun finally dropped behind Mt. Diablo, and the lavender ceiling shifted to purple; the patio next to the porch began to slowly fill up with couples.

La Bamba is a converted house with a porch in front and a small patio on the side where we were sitting. I saw Delbert and his wife take a table on the porch, out in front. She smiled, chatted, and laughed across the table from the sober-faced realtor. She didn't look like she was concerned about the murder. I wondered if he had even told her yet. Maybe I tend to judge things too much by my own experience.

Marti and I have been married a little over twenty-five years and like most older couples we know, we share just about everything. In working downtown, I have noticed that quite a few of the businessmen compartmentalize their lives. They seem to have a lot of things to do that don't involve their spouse, so it just stays that way. I suppose that might go farther than just time and events. Perhaps it becomes how they handle their money too. That's a little scary for me to understand. I guess I'm not built that way. How can you have a functioning marriage relationship if there are big private areas you have to constantly maintain? Why be so covert in your relationship? It must take a great deal of energy to keep it all going. Maybe that's why Delbert was so serious-looking.

I had told Marti about the high points as we rode in the truck, when I picked her up. She expressed concerns for my part in it (*she knew I wasn't guilty—thank you very much*) and for the other participants. Surprisingly, she was mostly concerned about the young policeman who was first to view the body. She kept talking about how shocked he must have been. As I listened I was watching Del while she talked and I wondered how he would tell his wife about the situation. If I remembered right, this was Del's second wife. His first had left him in the lurch, four or five years ago, for some sports guy, a tennis coach, or weight-room trainer. *Del and I have a very shallow relationship at best.* He had a very smooth, controlled look on his face. You would have thought he was explaining some investment to his wife, and since I couldn't hear, perhaps he was. Well, it was none of my business. I steered my fork into the food.

Thirty years ago, I thought I was a missionary—a *sign* missionary. I thought that I could affect change on the town through my work and my mouth. I tried to do every sign with a "what would Jesus do" attitude; each project was THE one, you know? I even signed my work with a verse address: Ephesians 2:10.

I looked for ways to involve the Lord in every job and conversation. It didn't take long for me to realize that the customers had more experience in messing situations up than I had at doing clever things with paint. I found too that there had been many, many well-intentioned hypocrites in the town's history. In fact, what I was told was that the hypothetical Christian businessman was the archetype of the town.

I'm sure that sounds jaded or disenchanted. It's not. I just found that all I can do is the best I can do. When it turns out well, I give God the credit. When things fall apart, as they sometimes do, I try to make it right and say I'm sorry. I take the rap. I don't know how else to do life. I make mistakes every so often, and sometimes, sometimes, there's no way to satisfy the client at all. That's life. There's always those few that are gaming the system, stretching our patience.

I meet a lot of folks in a year. Most don't let our conversation get below level three: *How're the kids?* I always hope for more sparkling success than I get, but a lot of people just want their privacy, I guess. Come to think of it, the Gospels don't show the odds being much better for Jesus's ministry.

"So what do the police think?" Marti was gently nudging me out of the clouds. She could see my mind had drifted away.

"They haven't got a clue. The big officer, Raddick, says it must have been an intruder. They found some scratches on a lower sash window in the back, and it was unlocked. I suppose they're checking all the homeless in the downtown area."

"But what would they be there for?" Her lips pursed in this cute S shape that she gets.

"That's the point. The whole place was empty. And then there's the wound."

"The wound?"

"Yeah. It was a ripped kind of cut."

"Not a regular knife-stab wound? You looked that close?"

"Well, not me, but the officer that went in first. He was babbling all about it when he came outside. Clare's neck was slashed too. Anyhow, the officer told me to forget what was said about the wounds. They want to keep that back, to use as a check when they question people. Just try to forget I said that."

"You don't think it was a burglar, do you?" She was looking at me with those piercing green eyes that had trapped me so long ago. Time hadn't dulled their power; those babies might as well be lasers. It was the sparkle in those eyes that had piqued my interest back then.

Marti tapped the plate with her fork. "You don't think it was a burglar. Honey, do you? Do you know who it was?" I just smiled back. "Oh, look." Marti was staring at the front of the patio where Lina was ushering some people toward an empty table. Lina's eyes and smile were fixed on the young man in the group. He was wearing an RJC jacket. He was a college man.

7

Just the Facts

I was back to driving the old Toyota pickup, Tuesday. Less flair, but more reliability and fewer rattles. I was kind of in a funky mood this morning, not looking forward to anything much. Even the smell from the spurting coffee maker didn't hold my attention like it usually does. I set up the two four-by-eight boards on the big wall easel and got the work orders out to see what was similar about them. They required different colors, but the subcopy could be the same color and that might save some time. I was thinking about the title words when the phone rang.

Got it by the third ring, "Signs by Vinnie."

"Vincent DiMora?"

"Speaking, how can I help you?"

"Mr. DiMora, this is Detective Bettencourt of the Riverglen PD. I was wondering if you could come down to our office and answer a few questions this morning."

"Is there any way you could come over here?"

"Where's that, Mr. DiMora?"

"To my shop, Detective. I'm working, but I can talk while I work. You dialed the shop number."

"Oh, the form didn't say it was a work number. I could have a car stop by and pick you up, if you like."

"What is the problem, Detective? I've had a business in town for twenty-two years. Surely, you know I'm the one who letters your department's cars. I'm dependable. I'm not going anywhere. Couldn't you come here?"

"Just a moment." I heard Bettencourt mumble to someone with his hand over the receiver, and then he came back. "My partner says he knows you, so maybe we can bend the rules a little here. May we come over right now?"

Stranger and stranger. Riverglen is still in many ways, a small town. I'm not in government, but it doesn't take much business around the city to meet most of the "force." We must have about twenty officers and maybe four detectives by now. I thought I knew 'em all. I'd never heard of Det. Bettencourt. Ah, vanity! Maybe Vinnie would learn something too.

I was taping off a panel (a painted shape to background and highlight part of the lettering message) on one of the signs when I heard their car pull up in front. The jingling bell announced the two men in sport coats. One was thin, and I recognized him from some work for Little League I had done last February. *Hazzerd? Harrard?* The other was thicker, his movements showing that it was not fat. He had black hair, cut very short, but brushed down. In high school, we used to call that a "college cut." He leaned an arm on the front counter and took visual inventory of the office. He was almost leaning on the "I'm working in back, come on back" sign.

"Vinnie?" the younger one yelled out. I finished smoothing the tapeline and picked up the lettering flat I had chosen.

"Come on back." I said in a normal voice over the low Dave Koz sax music I had going. They stepped around the counter and passed into the workroom. "You guys want some coffee? The cups are next to the machine." I started brushing in the panel with a dull red.

"Mr. DiMora, I'm Detective Bettencourt. I'd like to ask you a few questions about the Tribble death. I understand you were at the scene?"

"What's the matter, Detective?" His eyes narrowed. "Why do you ask that?"

"You seem on edge, Detective. You're talkin' so formal."

"I take murder very serious, sir."

"As should we all. But you're the first person to call me sir since I talked to Ms. Franklin's fifth-grade class on career day. That was several years ago. You just transfer in from Frisco?"

"Yes. How did you know?"

"Your sport coat. Nobody around here carries anything that nice. Last time I wanted a nice coat, I had to go over the hill to San Jose to get it. To answer your question, yes, I was 'at the scene.' Mr. Tribble had spoken to me at Eddie's earlier. He wanted a quote on some future signage in the lobby of the building."

"Mr. Tribble was the owner?"

"No, at least he said he wasn't. He wanted an idea of what it would cost to give to the prospective owners. That's what he said."

"Did you talk to him when you arrived?"

"Look, *Detective*, I understand your technique, and you don't know me at all. But I really don't see the point of the games. You know from the report that he was dead *before* I got there. You know that I *found* the body." He let out a sigh and wiped his hand over his face.

"I've seen the report, but I like to begin our interviews from scratch on things like this, sir."

"Okay, Detective Bettencourt, pull up a seat." I pointed at a stool with my elbow, and redipped the brush and began to paint again. "At breakfast, Clare—that's what we all called Mr. Tribble— asked me to meet him at eight thirty. I was about ten minutes late for the meeting, and I parked in front. The doors were unlocked, and I went inside thinking Clare was waiting for me. His Cad was parked in front. There was no one in the lobby, and I kept calling out his name as I went through the offices looking. I finally found him upstairs. I didn't touch the body, only the office door. Soon as I was sure he was dead, I called the dispatch." I said all this to the sign face in front of me as I brushed.

"The incident log says the call came from one Delbert McCaughey."

"Yeah, sorry. I guess it was Delbert that made the call. It was his phone. Del was in the lobby waiting for me. When I came downstairs, he was standing there, and he had his phone in his pocket. It seemed quicker. I was intending to use mine out in the truck, but he was closer."

"Mr. McCaughey was waiting for you too?"

"That's a funny thing, Detective. He made an appointment to get a quote on the same thing as Clare, but for the buyers. He had just arrived. I didn't want to say anything about it to Del when he made his appointment." *The funny thing was he was early, and I don't remember Del being early before, but I didn't want to say anything about that yet.* "It happens sometimes, see? You got two factions working on the same deal. If they both get the same quote, then I get the inside track on the job. I don't want to queer the deal, you understand?"

"So Mr. McCaughey didn't know about Mr. Tribble's interest in the building?"

"He didn't say, but he must have. He represented someone interested in buying and developing the building. I figured they were two sides of the same transaction." I turned and began to clean the brush, having finished filling in the panel. I washed it out in the thinner can and dipped the hair in oil and laid it down. "That insider stuff between realtors, I don't go there." I grinned. "I just do the signs, Detective."

I began to rough out the title line (For Sale) on the other sign with a Stabilo pencil. The detective was silent as I laid out the letters and taped the top and bottom edges. The other detective stood back, drinking my coffee and poking around into things on the counter. I mixed up some dark blue with a touch of gray and a little thinner, and rinsed out the flat again.

"Why do you do that?"

"It's full of oil. I don't want it in the paint. With that much oil, the paint would never dry."

"Didn't you just use it on the red on that sign?" Bettencourt pointed to the red panel.

"Yeah."

"Well, if you're going to use it in the blue next, why oil it?"

"Hmm, habit, I guess. Phones ring, people come in. It's easier to rinse a little oil out and way cheaper than buying a replacement brush if I forget it and it dried hard."

"What does a brush cost?"

"A good inch and a half flat like this is somewhere north of $30 now."

"How long does a brush like that last?"

"It depends. Several years, sometimes ten, fifteen. The older ones were made better. I have friends with twenty-five-year-olds in their kit that are still good. Use and care. Just like people, Detective. Use and care."

"Who do you think killed Mr. Tribble, Vincent?" He jarred me back into the interview. More technique, I suppose. Was this supposed to shake me up or did he really think I knew?

I turned and looked him in the eye. "I don't have the slightest idea, *sir*."

8

A Meeting of the Minds

In the silence after the door shut behind the detectives, my mind slowly filled with questions. Clare was known for risky projects, but he was also known for several major successes. Most of the ones that did well were on the fringes of town. I didn't remember any within the downtown area even though I was sure he had been on the "revitalization committees." The Downtown Redevelopment Committee, the Main Street Coalition, the Riverglen Historical Society—I forgot the names of the rest. It was all part of big business, I guess.

I'm not really sure what all they do. I've given presentations to a few breakfast meetings. All the folks spiffed up with what passes for power suits and ties, drinking coffee.

I get cynical, I guess. I suppose you don't really *have* to get dirty to do meaningful work. *Maybe.* Nothing ever came from those presentations and that anchors my attitude though. Just lots of talk and big, wide phony smiles.

So what had gotten Clare so interested in the Marchant building? It wasn't all that big, and he didn't seem very sure of his prospective clients when we had talked. Turning more farmland into another strip mall seemed more to his style. He had said there was an architect involved, which made the project seem pretty well advanced. I picked up the phone and punched numbers.

"Hey, good morning. Mr. Sinclare *in* this morning? Vinnie DiMora. Yeah, the sign guy. Thanks." Some more Dave Koz played. (I didn't know we had the same tastes.)

"Vincent! How are you?"

"Just fine, William, and you?"

"Good, good. Weren't the Monarchs hammering it out, Saturday?"

"Pretty well. They almost won it."

"Yeah, *almost.* That's the word. What can I do for you?"

"You heard about Clare Tribble?"

"Yes, yes. Fine man. Terrible thing, terrible."

"William, I was wondering if Clare had been working with you on the Marchant project. He told me there was an Architect involved."

"Why yes, we had done some preliminary sketches of the floor plan. They wanted to open up a few walls, combine some of the suites to give them a bit more space, nothing major."

"William, I know it's none of my business, but you know who the primary client was to be?"

"Well, I suppose it's not secret. Grierson Homes. They are moving their main offices from the bay area. The father passed away last year, and the two sons have decided to concentrate their new projects here in the valley, between Stockton and Fresno. Clare had talked them into settling in Riverglen. One of the brothers just bought the old Hedberg house. We're working on some minor renovation plans for it in the office right now."

I finished the conversation, hung up, and got back to work. That certainly answered that. Grierson Homes had been one of the bigger operations working in Northern California. I guess they had to run out of subdivision room in the bay area someday. Maybe those brothers could see it coming.

I got a little chill as I thought about it. *More subdivisions.* Eddie's would sure be buzzing when this leaked out. Farmland values would be moving up. Again. Traffic would thicken. We'd need more police, more firemen, more schoolteachers, and more schools too. This could have a big effect on Riverglen. I wonder if the mayor already knew. *They'd need more signs too, Vincent.*

The phone rang. "Signs by Vinnie, how can I help you?"

"Do you do pinstriping on trucks?"

"Sure do. I'll pinstripe just about anything!"

"We just bought a Chevy extended cab pickup? It's white, and I thought we needed to brighten it up a little. My wife drives it most of the time. She saw some of your work in the parking lot at Eddie's this morning. Can I come by and show you what we want?"

"Any time, eight to five."

"Great, I'll be right down."

I got most of "For Sale" painted and the phone rang again. This must be a latent Monday. This time, someone wanted a quote on a window splash (watercolor) sign, but they hadn't thought just what they wanted to say, so I had to spend ten minutes working it through with them. Finally, we got the job set, and I gave them a price. "Well, thanks. I'm just calling around to get an idea of what it will cost." They hung up. Enough of this stuff! I turned the answering machine on and went back to work.

People seem to think sign guys are some kind of information service. Like I do the signs as a hobby just to entertain me as I wait for the phone to ring. I have to turn over so much money each day, or I won't make it at the end of the month. They charge me for the electricity just like you. Then I stop myself. "I" don't really *do* anything much here. God does. I gave Him control of the business long ago. The strain of worrying about it was getting to me. One morning during my prayer time, I realized what the problem was, and I said, "Okay, You deal with it." I mean, who is better equipped for this anyway? Since then, I just do the work and bank the checks. I let the senior partner do the strategy stuff. (Incidentally, it's worked out better than I expected.)

A white Chevy x-cab pulled up in front and a guy got out. Tall guy. I cleaned my brush as the bell tinkled. "Be right there," I said and dipped it in the oilcan and hung it off the table edge.

He was well put together in modern cowboy chic. Mid-thirties, starched, long sleeved white shirt with a monogram, not common around here. Pressed jeans and white Nikes.

"I called about the pickup?"

"Sure, Vinnie De Mora." I stuck my hand out over the counter and got a firm grasp. "What did you have in mind?" His eyes were all over the office, looking at the examples on the walls.

"You have any pictures of your striping?" I pulled the big album from under the counter and plopped it open. He flipped through the pages, and I realized that many of the pictures were older than I had remembered. I really needed to tweak these books some.

"You've been doing this for a while?" He said this as he flipped the pages. I tried not to be sarcastic. Nearly everyone asks the same thing.

"About twenty-five years, give or take. What kind of work are you looking for?"

"The guy at the tire store said you do good work. I'm having new wheels put on this afternoon. I want something down the side, nothing gaudy. Maybe around the back too. What's that run?"

"Two lines around the truck would start at $120. Include the hood bumps and a little flash at the door handles and it's $160. Add some LA sponge work on the side and we're at $220. That's a common level for people to choose. I can use two nice pastels and a little brighter color in the flourishes to catch the eye. She'll be happy."

"Sounds good, what color? Maybe blue?"

"Blue's all right, but I do an awful lot of blue. What's on the interior?"

It went on like this until he was sure I wouldn't ruin his truck. Like practically everyone else, he finally told me to use my best judgment and go for it. We made an appointment for later in the week, and he left a $25 deposit. The name on the check was Grierson.

I looked at my watch and saw that it was after twelve, so I checked my pocket for cash and hung the "out to lunch" sign on the door and locked it. La Hildalguese is not an uncommon name around here. I thought it was a style of cooking (and it is), but it's a place, just a village in the mountains, like in the painting on the side of the truck next to the order window. I parked and got in line. You don't have to speak Spanish to order, but it helps. I speak "Flexican."

"Umm?"

"Un burrito, al pastor, con queso?"

"Grande?"

"Non, ordinor, por favor."

She shouted something untranslatable over her shoulder and looked back to the next guy over my shoulder. I stepped to the side and waited with the other vaqueros. No one talks in line; it's some kind of code, a kind of manly deed, this ordering of burritos. We all stand with our hands in our pockets looking tough. Well, maybe just a little knowing smile at each other now and then.

"Al Pastor." Not a question but a statement.

I stepped forward and handed the guy a $5. Now here's where it gets interesting. He counted out two ones and two quarters. I never know what to do. I pay with a $5, and I get different change every time. I tossed a dollar back. "Gracias!" I turned back to the truck. The menu said $3.25. My conscience was clear.

Back at the shop, I took the "lunch" sign down, got a tea out of the fridge, and sat down on a stool. Al Pastor is barbequed pork, spiced depending on which truck you get it from. These guys were pretty dependable. I prayed as I pulled the tin foil back from the folded tortilla. *Multitasking Vinnie.*

After work, Momma wanted Italian, so we went back downtown to our other hangout. Pasta! Pasta! was surprisingly *not* one of the busiest restaurants in Riverglen. When we arrived, there were several tables filled, but most sat empty. We took a place near the window and grabbed chairs. Marti said it had been a hard day at the shop. They had ordered a lot of specific flowers for a wedding later in the week, and the mart had sent the wrong "colour." You saw how I spelled that, didn't you? *Designers are fun.* (Colour?) Realities don't intrude on their worlds. *Enough.*

Marti said that she had been able to trade with four other shops in the general area, and their delivery guy had to drive all over swapping out the flowers. Which of course took the delivery guy off delivery, right? And then they got the call for an important funeral on short notice *(we're so sorry but we forgot to call you)*. I had a hard time being very sympathetic, and she began to heat up because of it. She knew I had shop gripes too, but this was her turn, and to not be sympathetic was not playing our game right. It had been a tragedy. She had solved the problem cleverly, but her boss didn't give her any credit for it (of course). I needed to look more concerned than I was. I struggled to find the right things to say, finding I'm not quite the master wordsmith that I think I am. Fortunately, the waitress interrupted us and then the servers; and by the time the main dishes came,

I think I was back on track. I told her what a great job she had done and how clever she had been (and lucky). She allowed as how she had conquered the problem and that things were now back to normal. I allowed as how things were never normal in either of our businesses, and her employer was lucky to have someone as smart as she to figure out a solution that quickly. She allowed as how I was right, and her smile crept back. And that smile, of course is the reason I live.

There had been a steady flow of cars along the street parking outside. There is another restaurant down the block and a new theater too. Being a car guy, I had idly noticed each one driving by. I caught myself watching a pickup pulling into a space while Marti was talking. I should have been looking at her the whole time. It was a white pickup like the man had driven today. A woman was driving. She was a little jerky but maneuvered the long truck into the space very well. It had new aluminum wheels, or at least, very clean aluminum wheels. The driver got out and the taillights blinked as she set the alarm and walked off. Nice looking with the kind of long blond hair that requires professional upkeep. Trim figure, tight designer jeans, fluffy pastel ski jacket, very expensive white running shoes.

"Eyes front, soldier!" I turned pink and snapped back to my bride.

"I just thought I knew the lady."

"Customer?"

"Maybe. Maybe her husband, I'm not sure."

"Your spaghetti's getting cold." Marti gestured with her fork.

Deep in the night, I woke to the darkness, sitting up with my eyes frantically searching the corners of the bedroom for I don't know what. Was it that marinara sauce? No. My stomach seemed okay., but my heart was racing like I had had bad coffee, and then the memory of the wet red wound on the body seemed fresh and pulsing, and overwhelmed me. The image flooded through my consciousness. I thought I could smell its fluids. I saw its vivid bloody red. I must have dreamed it.

Looking around in the darkness, everything was peaceful; there was nothing in the dark bedroom but Marti, snoring softly. Since I had been first at the scene, it seemed like I was intimately trapped in the crime, tied to the tail of the events like a cruel joke. I was just an innocent witness, wasn't I?

I sweated in the cool night air, and finally, I rolled out of bed and padded into the kitchen. As I poured a glass of water at the sink, I looked at the reflection in the dark window beyond. I sipped the tepid water and pondered just who that guy was. *Why was I mixed up in this? Why me, Lord?* I guess I was praying without knowing it. I could see my lips moving in the reflection. Praying automatically, a number dialed by my soul. *911.*

9

Straight to the Heart

Around ten the next day, I got a call from Del's assistant telling me that himself wanted to come over. I was working on the never-ending pile of bills. Every few days, I wrote what checks I could. I wondered about the call, but I supposed that it was the Marchant building coming back to life and that *business* must go on. He wasn't even ten minutes coming and that was a first for any realtor in this town. Growth was king just now, and they were the court princes with the attendant privileges. I heard the brakes on the tan Taurus scrinch to a stop. I closed the checkbook on my desk and stood up to the counter as he came through the door. In my head, I imagined "Hail to the Chief" playing, and I caught myself humming along.

"Good mornin', Vinnie." He stood patiently in his shiny suit and conservative tie.

"I heard at Eddie's this morning that you didn't waste any time getting cozy with the Grierson brothers." *I might have overstepped myself there.*

"Did you?" His smile went back into the closet, and the practiced business face flashed back on stage. I thought about my remark and realized there was no point in being obtuse.

"Seemed a little quick for some of the boys, I guess, but they are prospective clients." I artfully left myself out of the crowd. I'm too smart for that, of course.

"What did *you* think, Vin?"

"I'm not in your business, Del. I guess they were a sure thing for the building, murder notwithstanding. They were just waiting to be recontacted by somebody."

"Well, that's a realistic perspective. That's it in a nutshell. The Griersons are terrific people, so I called them this morning, early. I didn't call them until after Clare quit."

"So that's why you're here?" *He didn't quit, Del He died.*

"Yes, I was hoping you could bring me up to speed on the sign work so that I can be on the same page when I meet with the brothers this afternoon."

I smiled, "You're in luck then. Clare never got to talk with me. I have no idea what they want."

"Nothing?"

"Well, it wouldn't be hard to draw up something for you to talk from, but I don't have a budget figure to 'target.' You know there are lots of ways to spell s-i-g-n." (I must look out for myself. I told you before.)

"Can you give me some sort of ballpark figure?" He snarked at me with his toothy grin. Oh, I just hate it when I get the tables turned by a client like this. Ballpark figures are the noose that seems to fit your neck so very comfortably at first. Are you following the metaphor? I kept quiet, waiting for him to give.

Finally, he shook his head. "I'm thinking they'll want to keep it below $2,000, Vinnie. Their offices will take up the top floor. They like understated elegance—that's a big thing with them. Sort of implies you're getting more than you paid for."

"Like Corian instead of real marble, but not formica?"

"Exactly."

"When's the meeting, Del?" I looked over his shoulder at Felix, whose paw was at 10:30 a.m.

"One thirty. Can you give me something before then?"

"Can you give me a deposit, Del? You're asking me to set aside my work for the rest of the morning."

"How much?" *Always the bargaining. Be still my heart.*

"How 'bout a hundred? I've got two hours to do four hours' worth of work." *Thank the Lord for my computer.* He didn't even flinch. He pulled out his checkbook and wrote, said thanks, and that he'd be back around one o'clock.

The good news was that I didn't have any problem putting aside the two "For Sale" signs. And the really good news—the really, really, really good news—was that I had begun to lay out something for a building much like the Marchant building several months ago. That project had never happened. Someone had called and asked for a drawing, and I had stupidly started it without deposit. Of course, I never heard from them again. You'd think I'd learn this lesson, but I never seem to. *Is this the time for the paragraph expounding Romans 8:28. Can you look it up on your own? I'm busy telling a story.*

That job should be still in the computer, if I could just remember the title I had given it. Oh, yeah, it was a weird one, my sarcastic sense of humor working overtime that day. *BloodRed.dr* (.dr is a drawing suffix in my computer graphics program). It was going to be a doctor's office complex. These doctors were just out of residency in the big city back east. They thought red was classy (and it could be). A title sign next to the doors, an inside tenant directory, sample office door plaques—it was all there and close enough. The neat thing about the computer file was that that job had the parameters and borders already set up. All I had to do was change the spelling. The Grierson people didn't have a title for their project yet, though. I thought about it. It didn't really matter; everyone just wanted a target to shoot at during the first discussion. It had to sound local and historic, but nonspecific. The Marchant family had died out years ago, and the building never had developed much of an identity of its own. It was one of the few early twentieth century marble-faced structures still standing on Main. It had some fluting and pediments on the fascia. A little character, but not much. I thought of the dark vacant windows on the street, smiled and typed in something appropriate: "Heart of the Valley Offices."

10

As Suspected

And the evening and the morning were the third day, and it became Thursday. Now Thursdays are not always my friends. Sometimes, Thursdays mess up big time and make Fridays hellatious, and sometimes they don't. I knew that the "For Sale" signs better get done today, so I got hard after 'em, finishing before noon. I hadn't heard from Del after his meeting. I'd kind of hoped he would call. It might mean nothing, and then I thought that it might be wise to bank the deposit check soon. It's just business, right?

Not everyone applies the commandments to all they do, and I suppose that I don't do it like everyone else either. I have a theory about this. I think the Creator's purpose is the application of the law and not so much the words themselves. I think the law is our translation of God's thoughts into the culture we're stuck in, and that He is much more concerned with behavior than with strict obedience, but "Don't kill people" isn't too tough to understand. "Don't steal" might standup to a little adjustment here and there. You don't have to agree with me either.

After my chicken sandwich and Coke, I had several small projects to cut to size and coat out. By closing time, the drying rack was full. On Friday, I could letter till I dropped. I locked up and headed for the truck. Just as I pulled out of the lot, I saw someone getting out of a truck in front. White pickup with new mags. I remembered that he was coming Friday morning, so I stopped at the gate and got out.

"Vinnie! Were you just leaving?"

"Yeah, what's up?"

"Could I leave the truck tonight instead of bringing it in the morning?"

"Sure, let me open back up." I went to the front door, opened, and shut the alarm off. He was idling at the big side door as I slid it open and he drove inside.

The owner was all smiles. His creased jeans and sweater the epitome of country cowboy image.

"I realized it would be much easier for us if we left the truck here tonight. I hope that's all right?" I headed back for the front door with him trailing.

"Not a problem," I said, but something was tickling at the edges. We'd left the keys in the truck. I had a work order; what else was there? I pulled it off the wall where it was pinned. *Color?* "Mr. Grierson? Did you have any more thoughts on the color? I see we left our discussion to the interior colors, some purples and grays. That still okay?"

He stared over my head for a minute, looking at some other page. "Well, my wife mentioned she still wanted some blue in it." Still the strange stare. *Was he on drugs?*

"I can get some blue in it. Maybe in the sponged details?"

"Yeah, that'd be fine." He was looking out the front window, thinking about something else. "Well, see you tomorrow afternoon. Gotta hoof it." He went out the door and strode purposefully up the street. Strange guy; spacey but polite. Maybe it was the money. I locked up again and got in the pickup, thinking I should have offered him a ride. Maybe I would. As I pulled out onto the street, I saw a flash of the red and black sweater getting into a car up the street. Guess someone else offered him a ride. Mustang convert, dark purple (beautiful when it's clean.) That tickle again. What was it?

Marti wasn't home yet when I got there, so I began raking leaves off the lawn. "Fall is beautiful, but oh, you leaves." I had a goodly pile when it hit me. Clare's secretary had a dark mustang convert; I noticed it every time I passed his office.

Friday was, well, Friday. A couple of body shop fender repair stripes, and I did the white pickup. Chevys are pretty easy because the sides are so flat. I laid a quarter-inch tape as a guide for my fingers and striped them down the sides and across the back. A sponge flash highlight halfway down the side brightened it up and let me use a stronger color (purple). The blue and teal lines (I left the gray off) looked smooth together and then the erratic sponge work woke it up. I did a little simple design on the hood and the gate, a little "Von Dutch" design under the latch.

After lunch, I was able to work on the lettering like I had planned. I had a couple more body-shop repairs to do too. It's nice when the body shops bring their cars by. I'd go to them, but we're in the same neighborhood so it's no real bother. I spend more time matching the faded colors then I do striping.

Usually the gofer waits, and I get to know him a little. You learn some interesting facts about body shops. Who has to go to court because of poor business practices, who's into coke now, who thinks they are God's gift to auto painting, that kind of stuff. Fernando told me that his buddy Ricky (Reekie) was going to work for the Chevy dealer in town. He says he's excited to come to the states; he hopes to make a lot of money.

The body shops and the food processors are kind of a revolving door here. There is a constant stream of immigrants lining up to work, and although the pay is low, the benefits are good. I'll give that to the unions; they got the benefits that make it work for the young families. They are only here a few years, and then they go back. The blood runs strong, and the extended families cannot seem to stay separated for long.

Del finally called, saying the meeting had gone pretty well and would I come by Monday morning. He wanted me to bring a copy of the proposal so we could go over some changes the tenants wanted. I wondered if my truck owner knew what was going on. I wondered why he couldn't just talk to me himself.

At quarter of three, Mr. Grierson and the blonde came in the front door. Mrs. Grierson was all smiles and compliments as she walked around the truck. She giggled at the designs and said her friends would say she was a "hot rodder" now. I wondered if she had ever been a dancer. I gave Mr. Grierson the tag, and he peeled two hundreds and a twenty off his pocket roll.

"You were right, Vinnie. She loves it. Thanks." I gave them the regular warning about waiting to wash it and about waxing the striping in a few weeks. She climbed in and drove out of the yard, and he went back out the front to the car, a dark-green Jag sedan.

I finished the lettering a little early and decided to hit the yard again while it was still light. I locked up and headed home. The newspaper was waiting on the drive, and I picked it up as I walked to the door. Headlines stating that the police had a new suspect in custody, one Billy Martin. Mr. Martin was a homeless man who had recently been living in the alley behind the Marchant building. Mr. Martin's fingerprints had been found on and inside the downstairs window with the scratches. The police were holding Mr. Martin without bail. Sounded like they had good reason to.

11

911 Sign

Saturday, I worked on the '54, trying to get the wiring in order. I got excited when I first wired the dash and there were wires going all across the floor. I was trying to bundle them and get them arranged so when we carpeted it, it wouldn't be a bumpy mess. I had my head under the dash when Marti yelled at me. Of course, I raised my head and banged it. You know what's coming. By the time I got to the phone, everything was spinning. I said hello, and the electronic voice said, "Vincent! My window lettering is falling off! What are you going to do about it?"

"Who is this?" I answered through the fog.

"Minnie Cheever; Hearts and Flowers. You said this stuff would be good for seven years, and it hasn't made it through a month."

"Mrs. Cheever, I'll come by and see what the problem is." I hung up and looked at the icebox. I guess the pain was fading; an ice pack seemed like a lot of work. "Hon? I need to go downtown for a minute. Do we need anything?"

"You could get some milk. I think we're okay on everything else."

I dragged a denim work shirt on and grabbed the keys for the pickup. "I'll see you, babe," I said as I went out the door. I thought about the window in question as I putted into town. I had had to use vinyl letters on the window because the new display window was tinted, and I couldn't work on the inside. I had asked the owner why they were getting heavily tinted glass when they wanted people to look inside at the displays. Not only was tinted glass dark, it had twice the reflection to look past. She said that the glass shop had recommended it to the building owner and that it would make it cooler inside.

Hearts and Flowers was on Main, just down from the Marchant building, but on the other side of the street. The lettering in question was on the big front window. As I pulled up, I could see nothing wrong with the job. I got out and walked up to the window, wiping my hand over the edges of the letters. I couldn't find any problem, so I went inside. This would've been enemy territory for my wife, but to me, it was just another job.

The store was full of (six) customers. Hearts and Flowers catered to the young homemakers *(Can I still say that?)* and stocked lots of "country craft" items. Minnie was busy wrapping something in tissue, so I looked at some of the displays. Rusty tin roofing was big this year. You could cut it into just about anything; I noted. I saw a birdhouse that was kind of neat. It looked like an old farmhouse with a wrap-around porch. *Pretty sexy for birds*, I thought. Forty bucks. Well, it had a lot of work on it. Someone had cut doweling for spindles on the railing and glued it all together, and the porch was made of slats instead of one piece, so it had the turn of the century look, if you know what I mean.

I saw Minnie was finished, and I stepped up to the counter. "Saturdays always busy?" I asked.

"You bet they are, Vincent. But it doesn't help when people think my store is falling apart!"

Thanks for the polite intro, Minnie. "I looked at the lettering, and I don't see anything wrong. Want to point out the problem?" She sneered, slammed the register drawer shut, and stomped the way to the front. I followed and remembered that she hadn't paid me yet. Ding! When I gave her the bill two weeks ago, she had said she would send a check, which can sometimes mean thirty days in credit terms. She straight-armed the door, stopped and pointed at the corner of the F.

"I expected your work to last at least a year, Vincent. This just won't do."

I looked through the glass at the back of the F and still couldn't see anything. The window was in shade now, and the letters looked a uniform light grey of stuck adhesive. It is so easy to argue with some people. It's what they want, and their insecurity sets up all these arguments. It's the biggest challenge to step around. It always impressed me that Jesus, in the Gospels, speaks very directly but hardly ever gets into arguments.

"I'm sorry, Minnie, but I don't see anything wrong. Please point it out to me."

"Oh-h-g-g!" she muttered under her breath and banged the glass door open. She stamped her feet and pointed to the capital F. "Right there, see?" She reached out a manicured, overly long fingernail and scratched at the tail of the down-stroke a few times until she got the serif "worried." Then she pinched it and peeled it up off the glass. "See? It falls right off." Maybe I should hire her to do removals for me; she seemed to have the knack for it.

"I can replace that easily, Minnie, but someone must have been picking at the letter for it to come loose." I pointed at some marks on the white letter. "See where they scratched it? I'll replace it this time, just as a courtesy, but I warned you about being on Main Street. There is a higher rate of wear and tear here because of the foot traffic."

"I just didn't think it would come off that easily." *Ah, the sweet sound of truth, there.*

"Minnie, let's get it straight, shall we? It isn't "coming" off. Someone *picked* it off. Anyone could do that. Street people, school kids, customers, anyone. That's why I wanted to work on the inside surface in the first place, but the window's too darkly tinted. If the sun cooked the lettering some, it would stick better, but that'll take time. You only get sun for a couple of hours a day here." The buildings across the street were tall and blocked the afternoon light.

"Well, it cost a lot of money, and I want it to last."

"Speaking of that, I don't think I've received your payment yet."

"Oh, I'll be writing checks this week!" she turned to go back inside.

"I'll get to this Monday morning, first thing."

She stopped and stared at me. "You don't work on weekends?"

"By disappointment only, Minnie. I'll get it Monday morning, first thing." I left her and climbed back in the truck. I guess I could have gone to the shop and fired up the computer, but what difference would it have made to her, really? It was Saturday afternoon, and she wasn't open Sunday. I suspected she had picked at the letter herself anyway. There was something in her hand motions that made it seem sort of "practiced." I backed out of the parking and headed home, and an idea sparked. I turned at the corner and then turned again down the alley behind the old empty storefronts and the Marchant building where the murder had happened.

I stopped and shut off the truck by the blank back windows of the abandoned barbershop. There was a line of windows along the sidewall of the bottom floor, in a kind of weedy alcove between the buildings. They would give access to the main floor rooms, but because of the two-foot high foundation, the sills would be difficult to climb in without a ladder or a box or something. I got out of the truck and looked around. Downtown is sure quiet on Saturday afternoon. All our families were out by the freeway at the Big Box parking lots. They were selling used cars, or there was a carnival or something going on there today. I didn't find anything in the alcove except broken bottles hidden deep in the weedy grass. The new own-ers should plant something nice to look at here, maybe something thorny to keep the scavengers out. I went back out to the alley and looked around. There was a dumpster parked two buildings down. I walked over and raised the creaky lid, but the box was empty and I shut it as quietly as I could. I started to go back to the truck, and I felt someone looking at me.

That's an eerie feeling. The hair crawls on your neck. I turned around. A young man was sitting in the depression of the back door of one of the buildings right across the alley from the dumpster. His eyes glittered in the shadows. He was so dirty that he blended into the darkness. A smile appeared, and he gave a slight wave of his hand but he didn't get up. I waved back and went over. "Hello, brother," I said.

His family named him Samuel, but he said his street name was Speedy. At least that was what he said. I was not surprised at the nick name. He was smoking a short dirty cigarette that he had probably scrounged. Speedy knew who I was, though, so he must have been around the downtown for a while, and he was exceptionally polite. He said he respected me for my work and said he had a friend that was an artist. This was not what I expected to hear from someone who slept in alleyways. I asked him about it, and he said he liked his freedom, as if that explained it all. There was a telltale bulge in the side pocket of his filthy denim jacket. I thought he kept the cold at bay with something on the inside as well as another coat. I sat down on the asphalt next to him. I asked him about the day of the murder. I said I had read that the police had caught a suspect, and he laughed. He knew Billy, all right. He shared "finds" with him on occasion. Wine, cigs, blankets, they shared; they were brothers of the street. He said Billy'd be happy with a few nights in a warm cell.

Speedy said that Billy had a habit of finding spaces in vacant buildings to reside in. He had been using one of the closets in the Marchant building for the past month. Speedy felt trapped inside structures, so he left Billy to his "cribs."

He said the war had done that to him. I wondered which war he meant. It could have been the Gulf War, but it didn't make sense. Speedy looked too young. *Maybe we all fight a war.*

He smiled vacantly as he smoked and talked about the aliens that frequented the alleys around us. From his descriptions, he had failed to identify their origins. Maybe it was that war that was still going on in his head. He said Billy had worried one of the latches loose on the ground floor windows until it slid open, He just slept in the closets snug as a bug. Speedy said, "It was just his 'squat.'" They ate breakfast together at the mission at 6:30 each morning. They usually spent the morning collecting aluminum cans around the center of the city. It was safer to do that in pairs, he said. Some of the street people weren't so good at sharing the stuff they found, or at letting you find yours, so they watched each other's backs. The workers at the various chicken plants were well known for leaving a mess after their impromptu drinking parties in the parking lots after work. Actually, I guess Speedy and Billy were performing a public service.

Billy had been at breakfast on the morning of the murder, everything normal. After they ate, he went back to the "squat" for something, and they were to meet up later in the city park in the center of town. I asked him if Billy felt territorial about the closet. I wondered if Clare had surprised him, and they had fought. Speedy laughed. "Billy is the biggest wimp you could ever meet. You could take his underwear without a fight, if he wore any."

I drove home feeling that I had not accomplished anything. I wrote a reminder about Millie's letter on my clipboard in the truck so I wouldn't forget Monday and went inside. Marti and I watched a movie that night, and Sunday was textbook in content. It was actually satisfying when for once, nothing happened to break the rhythm of "the way it's suppos' to be."

12

Negotiations

Monday, it looked cloudy and we didn't usually get much rain in September. Even so, I scanned the skies as I drove. I decided to drive over to DelMac's office but first I cutout the letter to fix Minnie's window. I could do it on the way. I thought it would be best if it was done before she got to work. Hearts didn't open before ten o'clock, and it was just eight thirty.

The damaged letter came off clean. I positioned the replacement one carefully, rubbed it down tight, peeled off the transfer paper, got back in the truck, and drove over to DelMac Realty.

As I pulled into the curb, I noticed that dark purple Mustang convertible on the other side of the Taurus. I went in the front door, jingling the bell as I went, and stood at the front desk that was blocking the hallway. The office was like a comfortable living room—a sofa, upholstered chairs, a coffee table (with the requisite California Realty magazines fanned out), and a landscape painting of a storybook cottage about to be swallowed by out-of-control flower bushes. I'm sure it was a "collectable." I heard the swish of nylon and silk, and the resident secretary (*I'm sorry, office assistant*) came in.

"May I help you?" She said with a practiced smile. She was really a "stunner" to look at.

"I left a sign proposal for Del to look over."

"Mr. McCaughey is on the phone just now. Do you have an appointment?"

"He called and I came. I can wait." I sat in one of the chairs and tried to find a way out for those folks in that cottage. They might have to cut their way free. I knew that people were in there. There was smoke coming lazily from the chimney.

It was a long call. After ten minutes, I cleared my throat. "Do you think Mr. McCaughey will be much longer, ma'am? I really need to get back to work."

"Let me just check." She had been digging in her gargantuan purse. She wrote something down on a post-it, stuck it on her desktop, and then went down the hall. She didn't know me. I guess she was guarding the gate as ordered. She had beautiful auburn hair filled with fashionable red highlights. Nice blue eyes, trim figure. I had seen her before, but I couldn't place her. She came back. "It will be just a moment, Mr. DiMora." So she *did* know who I was. There was a buzz from the phone, and she picked up the hand piece. She made some mumbles and said to me, "You can go back now." She began tapping away at the computer and let me find my own way.

If it isn't clear by now, the office was a repurposed craftsman style house. Del and his partner had done a nice job of playing up what little features the old two-bedroom had and introducing some modern touches. The front windows were all new multi-paned vinyl units. They had a painted chair rail running down the hall, and the offices had simple paint treatments above it for individuality. Del was standing at his door and waved me inside his office. The walls were filled with pheasants and duck pictures, and there was a stuffed duck on the bookcase against the sidewall. I sat down. Every time a car went by, the sun off the windshield flashed into the room through the window and lit up the iridescent feathers on the duck. I was distracted and thought it was some kind of hunter's techno toy, and then I figured it out. It was a real duck, stuffed. Del wasn't that modern. He could barely use the computer.

"So Vincent, we will need a few adjustments." I opened the folder he handed me and laid out the drawings and the price-quote sheet, facing "himself." "Okay, to begin with—" and he began to gently tear the design apart. It took most of thirty minutes to get the gist of what was going on. The Grierson's had gone *way* beyond cheap. They seemed to have made it into a practiced art form. The sign design elements became so generalized until it looked almost as bad as our city logo. Then they graded down the materials until there was little left of that "understated elegance." I hardly recognized what we ended up with. It looked like it came from the ninety-nine-cent store.

"You're sure this is what they want?" I asked quietly. I never try to argue with the client at this point. I'll never get a true idea of where they're going if I do. The specs described what the local Walmart put up and threw away every month. Well, it was a business, not a debate. If I won, I might also *lose* big time. Then Del said something key. He said that he had met with the older Grierson brother alone. I should have asked what color his wife's hair was, or what he drove, but I buried my suspicions and left it alone. I would drop a copy of a revised drawing and price sheet by later. I got up to leave, and then I asked, "Who's the new secretary up front?"

"Oh, Margaret wanted to take some time off, and Clare's girl was certainly free, so I asked her to step in." He looked at me for a moment and said, "Do you think I was too quick? She seems awfully good at her job."

"I don't know, Del. Not my business. Good help is hard to find these days." I covered it up with my "award winning" smile and headed back to the shop. I never got good grades in Math in high school. I couldn't produce the right answer under pressure. This made for an interesting equation though. Margaret was close to retirement, I guessed.

At the shop, the answer machine was for once, full of messages. I called several clients back and was rewarded with a couple of sign orders, a car to stripe, and a couple of meetings scheduled. Not bad for a Monday. I decided to celebrate with another *carne asade* burrito and drove over to my favorite taco truck. When I got back, there was another blink on the machine. I pushed the button as I chewed. I listened to Detective Bettencourt tell me he wanted to talk again, and I called his beeper number. He called right back.

"Vincent? Can we come by this afternoon?"

"Sure, Detective. I'll be here till five." *I wonder what that was all about?*

13

Burritos and Boats

I was lettering an 8-foot banner when they came in. It was only two o'clock, so it hadn't taken long for the boys to drive over. The detective ambled over to my side, and his partner pulled out one of my portfolio albums onto the counter and began to study the photos.

"What kind of paint are you using there?"

"Is that a casual question or are you on special assignment with the Sign Police?" I smiled. He still wasn't sure how to take me. I thought it was funny; maybe it was too much of an insider's joke. The Sign Police are real. They're a group of sign guys that note some of the terrible choices people make on their signs. They often show the photos in the trade mags. They are constantly writing up articles for the trade. It's tough to get ahead of all those brothers-in-law and college art students. "It's enamel, Detective."

"Oh, I thought so. I smelled it when we came in."

"I don't even notice the smell anymore."

"I had a boat where I was before. I had to paint the name on the transom. I used something like that stuff. Dried really shiny and hard. I had to change the name before I sold it. It was a pain to get that old stuff off."

"What'd you use?"

"Oh, I had some rubbing compound. Took me most of a day to get it off. Then I had to revarnish it again."

"What was wrong with the name?"

"At the other department, my nickname was Ratty. I called the boat the Rat Hole."

"You mean like 'a boat is a hole in the water you throw money into?'"

"Yeah! I didn't think you flat-landers would understand that."

"We're not always as dumb as people think, Detective. What did you change the name to?"

"Sea Change. That way, it would sell easier, at least I thought so."

"When was the divorce final?" There was silence, and finally, I turned around. He was smiling thinly at the floor. I paletted my brush and did the last two letters.

Finally he spoke up. "It shows that clearly?"

"I just put two and two together." I went over to the table, washed the brush out, and oiled it.

"Maybe we should exchange jobs." He smiled broader and changed the subject. "I wanted to run something by you, Vincent."

"Call me Vinnie, *Ratty.*"

"Okay, Vinnie, but no one calls me that here." I saw a patient smile. "When you got to the Marchant building, did you park out front?"

"Sure, right next to Clare's Seville."

"Vinnie, this is important. Were there any other vehicles parked there?"

I had to think. I usually notice things like that. I didn't remember any other cars. The streets were pretty bare that early. There might have been a pickup at Stacy's across the street, but I'm not sure. Stacy's is a bar (actually, the only bar on Main street). There are usually regulars who stop in for their liquid breakfast. He hadn't mentioned Del's Taurus. Of course, I didn't see it until I went back outside.

"No, I don't remember any other. What's up, Detective?"

"Well, we have a witness that puts another automobile there at the projected time of the murder."

"And?"

"Well, Vinnie, I shouldn't say anything, really. He's not the most credible witness. His description was vague at best. I was hoping to you could corroborate it."

"O-o huw, I love it when you speak: *Detective!*" He almost smiled. "If I could remember anything, I'd sure tell you."

You're probably thinking that I should have told him about some of the other stuff I'd observed so far. I thought about it, but it seemed to be a well-run investigation, and I didn't *really* know anything substantial at this point. Police officers don't appreciate junior detectives even if they could spell words like "corroborate." I have found that professionals like to be "in charge." To have someone outside the ring of authority come up with important information is threatening to them. It's their job to figure it out. Besides, it wasn't my business to say anything. I didn't want him to think I was poking around in his case. I didn't know if I knew anything important anyhow. I'm just the sign guy, not a sleuth.

There wasn't much more to say and the fuzz left. I cleaned off the pencil marks on the banner and did some computer work until closing time. The phone didn't ring once. I locked up and got in the truck. I decided to swing up Main Street on the way home. The streets were bare of cars, but the west-side high schoolers were making their after-school migration back home. Groups of guys and girls paraded down the sidewalks toward the hood, hooting at each other and laughing. I guess I was like that at one time, but I sure couldn't remember. How can they walk with their pants so low? Inquiring minds like mine want to know these things. As I passed the scene of the murder, I caught the "sold" sign in the window of the front office. Del wasn't telling me everything either, was he? I took a chance, flipped a left, and cut back up the alley to the parking lot behind the building. This lot served the whole block of stores, not just the two-story Marchant building. I got out and walked quietly into the alley behind the rest of the block.

I wondered if the detectives had interviewed all those kids walking by that morning. They would have been earlier, but they might have seen something. It would be a horrendous task though, and kids that age wouldn't be too helpful.

I didn't see anyone in the alley, in the doorways, or around the dumpster (or in it). The other side of the alley is the side of the old California Savings Bank, long gone. I reached the sidewalk at the end of the alley and turned right. That bank building has been occupied by several "public" tenants since the bank moved away. It was currently vacant again, and securely locked up. There was an outside concrete-on-steel staircase leading to a few second-story offices. I had to make signs to warn off skateboarders from going up and down the heavy stairs. I thought about the floorplan as I went up the stairs. The offices were laid out in an "ell" with a corridor access to the restrooms in the corner. They were one-room offices. The cheapie tenants came and went, start-up operations that quickly outgrew the space.

I went to the short dark interior corridor off the corner and called, "Speedy?" There was no answer, so I went farther into the dark. There was a ceiling light at the end of the hall, but it wasn't working. I called out his name again. The restroom doorways were around a corner, the men's straight ahead and the women's to the right. I could just make out something on the floor at the end; my eyes were slow to adjust to the dark. I shut one eye and called out again. "Speedy?" The lump of shadow moved a little. I opened my eye, and I could just make out the ragged jean jacket and the old tennis shoes.

"Yeah?" The voice was hoarse and breathy, betraying his habits.

"It's me, Vinnie, the sign painter. Remember?" I stood back against the corner wall so the light outside painted me. I had him trapped, and I didn't want to frighten him.

"Vinnie? Vinnie the Brush? You that guy?" He rolled upright and pulled himself into some semblance of order.

"You okay? You need something?

"Nah! I just decided to take a nap. It's quiet up here after the offices close."

"Can I ask you a question about that morning? You got me thinking the other day. It might help your friend, Billy."

"Sure, sure." There was the flare of a match, and he lit a cigarette stub. "What's up?"

"Did you sleep up here the night before?"

"Yeah, 'sit a prob?"

"Not to me. What time did you go down to find Billy? Any idea?"

"Hmm, it must have been early. Like I said, he wasn't in his crib. He was in the alley by the dumper. We went over to the home, and breakfast wasn't ready yet. They serve at seven thirty. Had to've been between seven and six thirty. I don't gots a watch, but it must've been."

"Okay. Just one more. Did you see any cars parked in the lot back here?"

"Aw, I don't remember that kinda stuff, Vinnie. I was *just* up, and I was lucky to find Billy. I'm no good without my coffee. I don't remember even looking out in the lot. I was looking for Billy. That's all."

"Hey, no prob, Speedy. I'll go. You need anything?"

"Nah, I got everything I need right here." He smiled and patted a lump in his coat pocket.

As our dinner enchiladas cooled down, I brought Marti up-to-date on all my conversations. She said the local gossip had noticed Del's piracy. (Well, it wasn't real *piracy* exactly.) The secretary's name was Ginnie, Ginnie Soares. She had worked for Clare for two years, came right out of junior college. I thought about that and the near-new Mustang.

Some people just fall into it, don't they? When you work for yourself, or by yourself, you can slide into jealousy easily. The Bible says the rain falls on the just and the unjust alike, but sometimes it seems like the unjust get a little more of that water, sometimes. Course it wasn't fair to say that at all. I didn't know anything about Ms. Soares. She might be a truly wonderful person—snooty but competent.

"Are you all right, hon?" Marti was evaluating me across the table. I told you the power that those eyes have.

"Yeah, I was just thinking. Sorry."

In the truck, Marti smiled and asked about next Wednesday. It took me a second, but she noticed I hadn't jumped on that it was her birthday.

"So you don't have anything planned?" She was casting and beginning to troll.

"Why, is it important? Something I forgot?" Sometimes, the best defense is an active offense. She didn't say anything more, but I knew I'd better not foul up. It was a warning shot across my bow.

14

The Other Detective

Tuesday morning, I got Del's new stuff worked out. I found a nice little graphic of an acorn and leaf, and used it to dress up the designs a little. It was simple but elegant, and I could paint it, cut it out of something flat, or carve it in three dimensions and attach it. I printed it all out and a new price sheet, and put it in a folder. A truck was coming in today, and a little after nine o'clock, it showed up. Mr. Fletcher owns a local plumbing and air conditioning business. This made the fifth truck I had done for him, but he still felt he had to come over and dictate the specs.

"Hey, Vinnie!" He smiled and sauntered up to the counter. "Got the new truck out here. What'chu gonna put on this one? Nothing gaudy, I hope." *How could you possibly make Fletcher Plumbing gaudy?*

"Anything different on this one, Mr. Fletcher?"

"You got a picture of the other one? You remember it? Do it just like the last one. Plumbing and Air Conditioning, that's the ticket." I had photos, drawings and the patterns carefully stored.

"No problem. You can pick it up tomorrow around noon."

"Here's the keys." He flipped them on the counter, and I picked them up. I watched him climb into the accompanying pickup, and I went back to open the barn door and pull it around inside.

It was almost noon by the time I got the patterns dusted on the truck, and my head ready to do the lettering. I thought I would drop off the folder with Del's new drawings and get something to eat before I really got to work on that truck. I set the machine, locked up the shop, and got in the pickup. Traffic is usually busy on Tuesday because of the flea market just outside of town. I try to avoid the busy streets leading there, so I cut across the industrial section and wound up on Main again. There were lots of women and small children walking the sidewalks and looking in the furniture store windows. I should mention that even with all the vacancies, there are at least five furniture stores downtown. It's becoming epidemic.

Del's car was gone, but the Mustang was there, so I parked and went inside. Ginnie was busy tapping on the keyboard.

"Oh, hello." She had long painted nails, and I wondered how she managed the keys.

"I have the revised drawings for the Grierson project." I laid the folder on her desk. "I saw a sold sign in the window this morning."

"Yes, we were late in getting it up. Mr. McCaughey posted it yesterday after the police cleared the building. They wouldn't let us in until they were through, you know."

"I hadn't thought about that. I guess they had to keep it closed."

"You know, I heard they found fingerprints of some homeless guy in the room where Mr. Tribble was stabbed." I had gone from outsider to insider in one blink of her long eyelashes.

"Where'd you hear that?"

"From some of the girls who were talking at lunch. Mr. McCaughey was real excited when I told him about it. I hope they catch the guy that did it soon. Everybody who works downtown is worried." She was leaning forward in a conspiratorial pose. Her dress's neckline drooped for a view that I quickly looked away from. Surely, she wasn't that naïve.

"Yeah, I hope so too."

I motored over to the roach coach for lunch. *Who said it was a guy that stabbed Clare?*

Around two thirty, the front bell rang and someone came in. I was on a stool, lettering on the air conditioning van, and I didn't want to turn around. "Can I help you?" I said as I finished "Conditioning."

"I have a problem with the truck." I turned around, and it was the blonde that I presumed to be Mrs. Grierson.

"Sure, what's the problem?"

This kind of thing always gives me tingles. The project never looks as good as when they first see it. Sometimes to the customer, it looks different the next day (or the next week, or the next month). We went out front to the big white Chevy parked at the curb.

"There are blue marks all over it." I looked at the striping and saw the blue Stabilo (water-soluble marker) that I use.

"You mean these?" I pointed at two of the marks.

"Yes. What can we do about them?" Her hands on her hips.

I went back in the shop for the spray bottle and a rag. One shot of 409, and they wiped right off. She looked deflated that it was so easy. "That do it, or is there something else?"

"No, everything else is perfect. I didn't know they would come off so easily."

"Hey, I probably forgot to say something when you picked it up. I couldn't wipe them off then because the paint was still sticky. I'm sorry I didn't mention it, Mrs. Grierson. They go away when the truck gets washed."

"Thank you again, *Vincent?*"

"Yeah, *Vinnie*. Your husband bought the Marchant building? You folks moving here to stay? I heard you were from the Bay area."

"Yes on all counts." She smiled and looked around at the street of surrounding businesses and then at my door. "I may be back to talk with you, Vinnie. I do a little decorating, and I might just set up an office downtown. I would want something a little more elaborate than the Grierson brothers."

"Sure, anytime." She smiled, waved, and got in the pickup.

Tuesday night is Chinese for the DiMoras. The Golden Dragon was buzzing, and the windows steamy from the hot food. The always-smiling Chinese girl brought our Mu Goo Guy Pan and rice, and smiled herself over to another table. Marti served us up with the wooden paddle. The first smell of Chinese cooking is always what gets me. Wow! I dug in with my gaijin fork.

"I heard something interesting today, hon." Marti is a dainty eater and can talk while she eats. When I do, it gets embarrassing.

"You did?" I mumbled between bites.

"Several of us downtown get together for lunch and guess who joined us today?"

"Hilary Clinton?"

"Be serious!"

"Why? Michelle Obama?"

"Honey! It was Ginnie Soares."

"Clare's former secretary."

"Yes. She was a fount of information. Who's doing what and who's not, but she said something very interesting."

"Yeah?" I hadn't stopped forking yet.

"She said that Clare Tribble had quite a falling out with Gene Sorenson over the Griersons." Gene was a very able contractor in town. His projects kept getting bigger and more ambitious.

"He's the one building Valley View Estates, isn't he? The ones with the over-sized lots?"

"Yes. Ginnie said that Clare was a big help with his financing the last two years, and since he met the Griersons six months ago, he kind of left Gene in the lurch."

Helping them establish an office here wouldn't endear him to *any* of the local builders, would it?

15

Love Notes and a Power Lunch

Wednesday morning, I woke with a nagging hunger. I bought a couple of donuts on the way in to supplement my coffee. I thought about Sorenson while I waited for the shop coffee pot to perk. I hadn't had much to do with Gene Sorenson since he went "big time." When he had built "spec" houses and he needed a "better" sign out front, I had been his man. But once he began the subdivisions, he switched to one of the bigger sign shops in Stockton.

Subdivisions are fun because you do several applications adapting the same theme—title sign, model titles, walking directionals, off-site directionals, and so on. A whole package. It was production work. Everything to set the scene for the "new look" that the houses' design could create. Even the decorators get involved. But Gene got into Stockton society about then and began dealing with the bigger suppliers in the building trades. He made new friends and forgot about his old ones, I guess, so I had lost touch the last few years.

I had a lot of phone calls to make this morning, and I stopped brooding about it. When Mr. Fletcher came for his not-gaudy truck, I asked him about Gene.

"Oh, *Gene.* He and I used to do a lot together. I got all of his pipe and ductwork, and I still do some of it. He's gotten *bigger* now. Subdivisions aren't my thing, you know, Vincent. I'd need to hire lots of guys and another foreman to run them. I'd spend most of my time in the office on the phone gripping to suppliers. I don't want to grow that much. I like being out on the job-sites with the guys. You have no idea the troubles that growth leads to, Vincent. Say, why did you ask about Gene anyway?"

"Oh, I just wondered, I haven't seen him for a while."

"He was at Eddie's just last Monday for breakfast. You didn't see him then?"

"No. When was he there?"

"Sure, he came around the time you left, sat right at the counter next to—what's his name, Tribble, the guy that got his self killed?"

I didn't say more than goodbye and got back to work. About fifteen minutes was all I could take. I punched in some numbers and held the phone to my ear. "Detective Bettencourt, please. Hi, this is Vinnie. Excuse my asking, but did you guys trace Clare back to Eddie's? You did. Did you talk to the guy he was sitting next to, after me, that is? No? Gene Sorenson. S-O-R-E-N-S-O-N, yeah. A contractor that used to work with Clare a lot. Yeah, used to. Hey, you're the detective. Sure, glad to help." I hoped I hadn't gone too far. It's hard to know when you're meddling and when you're being helpful, isn't it? There's a very thin line.

I worked as late as I could and then headed downtown to Heart's. I went in, picked up that clever birdhouse, and plunked it on the counter. Minnie smiled broadly, agreed that it was such a special piece, and said she would wrap it for me. It was too weird a shape for a box so she tied up tissue around it with a ribbon and added curls and all that girly stuff. When she was done, I asked her to take it off what she owed me as she hadn't written the check yet. She was fine with that, and I carried the package out to the pickup. As I sat behind the wheel, I looked at the block of windows across the street. It was sad looking around at what could be and wasn't. Maybe the Grierson's offices would spark some growth here. I sure hoped so. I had a few short stops to make and then on home.

Marti was whistling from inside when I went in the back door. She was setting things out on the counter for dinner. I came up behind her and hugged her close. "Whacha doin', Sa-weee-tee?"

"Getting dinner ready, trying to figure what we'll have," she said.

"I thought Wednesdays we usually did Mexican?" I whispered in her ear and hugged tighter.

"Well, we could," she giggled.

I went into the closet and picked out something better than my paint-daubed jeans and a nice knit shirt. She was watching from the hallway.

"You're serious?"

"Sure," I said. "We ought to celebrate." I waited a beat. I heard her go in her closet. "I got a big job in today." There was a groan and she hissed, "*Men!*" under her breath.

La Bamba was rocking by the time we got there. We were later than usual, and they had had to set up several tables in the center of the patio to handle the extra crowd. We waved hello to some friends as we were led to one of these center tables, a little one. Lina brought chips and took our orders. We were surprised at all the people and the infectious current of emotions from the patio crowd. There was a flock of high schoolers laughing and shouting at each other. I guess we were like that once, but again, I sure don't remember it. I've always been very reserved and polite, *always. I'm sure I was then.*

The enchiladas came and we devoured them. Soon, we were scraping at the plates with our forks. "Well," I said, "do you want to see what they have here for dessert or go for yogurt like usual?" I studied the check and reached for my wallet. Marti smiled shyly.

"Whatever you want," she said, and I nodded slyly as Luiz took the check. There was a fanfare of guitars from the kitchen alcove and four guys marched out, singing something in Spanish and giving that wild catcall they love to do. They headed right for us, and one of them plopped a red sombrero on Marti's head as they began to sing "Happy Birthday" (still in Spanish.) By the time they reached the end, everyone in the place was joining in and laughing at Marti's face which now matched the sombrero. Luiz brought us a big bowl of flan with lit sparklers stuck in it. Marti had to wait for them to go out and for the wires to cool before we could taste it. It was like very sweet tapioca and with the golden crust, just perfect. She had that smile on now, and I thought I had maybe come a little closer to the center ring on the target. At least I had made it past the outer ring. *It changes every year, you know, and it's hard to know when you've got it right.* I got up and thanked Eduardo and the guys for their part. I handed the envelope to her as I sat down. "What's this?" she asked.

"I don't know. Luiz gave it to me for you. Open it." She did and unfolded the card inside.

"Looks like we have to go to the yogurt shop after all," she said. So we did, and the library (in her favorite book on the shelf), and the gas station (taped to pump number 3), and the grocery store (her favorite checker), and home. She jumped out of the car before I got it in the garage and disappeared through the front door. I finally caught up with her in the backyard, unwrapping the birdhouse where I had hidden it. I hid it under the patio table before coming in after work. I made some coffee, and we sat on the swing sipping and looking at the autumn stars. Even though it was cool out, we kept warm enough. We had had twenty-six years of practice keeping warm.

❧

Thursday was tough. No way could it measure up to the night before. The phone didn't ring, and I finished all but one of my work orders. I was about to go out for a sandwich when the phone rang—twice. The first call was from Detective Bettencourt.

"Vinnie! You'll never guess whose prints were on that office door next to yours."

"Whose?"

"Did you know you have to be fingerprinted to get a state contractor's license?"

"No-o-o-o."

"Well, Mr. Sorenson did, and he was in the room before you."

"How do you know that?"

"Your prints overlap some of his."

"Whoa! Nice work, Detective."

"Nice tip, Vinnie. We're going to pick him up right now for questioning. See ya."

Now there's a piece of information I didn't expect to learn. I stared at the receiver and then hung it up. Then the phone rang again.

"Vincent? Bill Grierson. Hey, I'm really sorry I didn't put it all together the other day. You must think I'm some kind of stuffed shirt. I never thought much about the proposal Del was getting until I looked at it. Could you come over and talk about it?"

"Sure, Mr. Grierson, anytime."

"Have you had lunch?"

"No, actually I was just going out to get something."

"Well, why don't you come over here? We're working out of a bedroom in the new house until we get the proper office set up. Adele could make us some sandwiches, and it could be a working lunch." I told him that would be fine.

Whoa! A new suspect and a power lunch all in one morning. Could it get any better?

16

The Other Half

The house was a four-bedroom with a three-car garage, about as big as we offer in Riverglen. I'm sure they had twenty acres of almonds somewhere, just out of town, where there was space behind the trees for the dream house to be started. They could afford it, but for now, they had a nice tract house. It was the smart thing to do.

I pulled up to where the x-cab was in the driveway. Mr. Grierson answered the door at the first ring. He must have been waiting for me. Mrs. Grierson waved from the kitchen, and we proceeded into a study with a roll-top desk and a computer. He motioned, I sat in a nice, upholstered leather chair and he sat in the swivel seat at the desk.

"I think I screwed up at first, Vinnie. I let my brother take that meeting with Del, and he got the whole thing wrong in my estimation." I smiled politely and let him talk.

Where in the world was this going?

"See, we'll be interviewing all kinds of people at the office, from decorators to painting contractors even the financial people we link up with. If any of them get the idea we're cheap to the point of poor quality, well, there goes the project. Can you see what I mean?"

"You want the "quiet elegance" to have a more capital *E*?"

"Right! If we look *cheap,* we won't get the right people on our team. It's a volatile market out there right now." Mrs. Grierson called from the kitchen (on the intercom, *woohoo*) that lunch was ready. We got up and went back through the living room to the French doors giving out to the patio. The table was really quite impressive. Mrs. Grierson had prepared a Chinese chicken salad with "shivers" of almond (*Marti never could say slivers, she always said shivers*) and sesame seeds sprinkled all over the exotic lettuces. I smelled bacon in it too. There was garlic bread, fresh from the oven, covered with a checkered cloth.

"Please, Vinnie, sit sit." She smiled and waited until we were both sitting and stood back by the French door. "What would you like to drink, gentlemen? Coke, beer, water?"

"Water for me, hon," Mr. Grierson said.

"Water's fine," I added.

What do you do when you're at someone's house and they don't pray before eating? I listed the possibilities in my mind and picked the least convicting choice, praying quickly and silently, just a nod of the head. *Hey, I don't know these people.*

Mrs. Grierson brought out three glasses with ice and a pitcher of water, and sat down with us. The salad was terrific, and I told her so. I should know; I had two helpings. She said it was quick to fix and her husband loved it. Well, I did too. I thought it tasted a little different and asked her about the taste. She said she used almond oil instead of the canola that the recipe had asked for.

"Wow, what a difference," I said. "Funny, this being an almond producing area, I never thought of almond *oil.*"

"It's on the super's shelves if you look."

"I guess there's a lot right under my nose if I looked." We laughed and enjoyed the salad.

After eating, we got to specifics, and I suggested several changes we could make to make the signs look richer and more in keeping with the architecture: a little faux marble, a few dimensional details. Actually, they were all of the details that had been removed. He liked them all. *That was easy.* He asked for a loose (*here we go again*) budget figure, and I picked a number higher than I thought it should cost, just to be safe. He said fine and went to get the checkbook. *What a guy!*

I asked if I could help clean up the table, stood, picked up the plates, and followed Adele. She smiled a thank you, and I followed her through the French doors into the open kitchen. As I laid the plates in the sink, I saw how orderly the kitchen was laid out.

I go into this now because my first impression of her had been, well as kind of a bimbo, a Barbie doll kind of woman. I could see there was much more to her underneath the makeup. I commented on the plate pattern as Marti's boss had picked the same pattern when she got married a few years ago. Adele said it was something they had bought together early in their marriage. She asked about Marti, and I told her a little about us. She really seemed interested.

"You can't know, but that's one of the real reasons we moved here from the Bay, Vincent. San Ramon got to be such a rat race, all so pretentious. We wanted to begin again, make new friends, and grow into some community instead of feeling like an accessory."

"Well, there's room to grow here for sure. Get Del to take Mr. Grierson, uh, Bill, to Rotary Club. It's a joke in some towns, sure, but in Riverglen, it's a real force for good. There are lots and lots of projects, and some very neat people that belong. They meet for breakfast above Eddie's every Tuesday morning."

"Are you a member, Vinnie?" Mr. Grierson was standing at the end of the counter, holding the check he had written.

"Oh, I used to be, but it got to be too much for a one-man shop operation. I need to be at work every morning, it seems. But I think you'd like it just fine." It was then that he handed me the check, and as I reached for it, I glanced to my left, at the knife set in the wood holder standing on the counter by my elbow. "Thanks. Lose a knife?" There was one steak knife missing from the otherwise full block.

"Yes, that's a funny thing. That happened right after we moved in. One got misplaced," she giggled. "That set is kind of sentimental to us. Bill's brother gave it to us at our wedding. I think he bought it off the TV or something," she said the last part behind her hand.

"Well, he meant well, honey." Bill smiled in a reserved way. "He just doesn't like to pay retail."

"We're afraid to throw it away because he comes over here all the time to use the office in the bedroom. We wouldn't want to hurt his feelings."

I said goodbye and began my exit. Mrs. Grierson made me call her Adele. I paused at the porch steps. "Are you serious about meeting quality people in town?" They both nodded. "I've got an idea you might like. Why not come to church with Marti and me this Sunday? We could introduce you to some folks. There's no obligation, just a visit." They said they'd think about it, and I left. The check was for more deposit than I had expected; and I was elated about having the Griersons, sorry, *Bill and Adele*, as new clients and maybe, maybe even as friends.

17

The Word from the Alley

Friday, I went to work happy again. I had a future project (and a check), and I needed to begin gathering materials. Marti and I had prayed about the Grierson's coming with us to church. It was, however, a wait-and-see proposition at this point, and they could very well have been just polite with their answer.

I got several Friday, body-shop touch-ups to do, and the day filled up. Just after noon, I got a call from Adele Grierson saying that they would like to go with us to church. I told her where to meet us and set lunch plans afterwards with a call to Luiz. On Sundays, the patio fills up quickly, so you needed to make a reservation. The phone rang again as soon as I hung up. It was my new best friend, Detective Bettencourt.

"So, Vinnie, I think we'd better get you a badge or deputize you or something."

"Really? Sorenson didn't have a good explanation for you?"

"Worse than that, his friends at Eddie's remember the argument they had at the counter. It was a duzie."

"Wow. I didn't hear anything about that."

"People don't like to share things like that, Vinnie. If it had been a fight, they'd talk; but an argument, well, people think it's private or subject to individual interpretation. They don't say anything unless you know to bring it up. We're going back to everyone that might have seen or heard anything." He paused. "I think this guy's a strong suspect, Vinnie."

"Well, as much as I like Gene, he does have a temper. I hope you get it all figured out."

There was a long pause. I could tell he wanted to say something else but didn't. I had a few questions too, but I didn't want to dig into his investigation or question his casework. I said goodbye and hung up. I finished the revised Grierson drawings, and since it was 3:30 p.m., I locked up and headed home.

I got a head start on the yard that afternoon, and Saturday morning, I used the extra time to mess with the wiring in the '54. That felt good. I even fit the new rubber door seals on. The doors now latched with a click and a muffled *chuff* when I gave them a shove. On a ride around the block, I found that the rattles had substantially diminished. I felt pretty good. After spending many a night adjusting the hinges back and forth, trying to get the door centered in the door frame, I had just about given up getting it right. Parked in the driveway, I must have been daydreaming about success. Marti shaking me was the next thing I remember.

"Hey, Hotrod Man, you had a phone call while you were cruising the hood."

"Oh." I got out of the truck and shut the door with a *chuff* of the new rubber. "Hey, babe, listen to this." She stopped in mid-step and turned around. I opened the door again and shut it. *Chuff.* She made a *hmm* sound and went back into the house. Oh well, maybe it wasn't going to bring world peace; but it was still a big deal to me.

The phone number I called back was one I didn't recognize. It rang a long time. I let it go eight or ten rings and hung up. Funny. Why call and not be there? Well, I might have misdialed, so I tried it again. This time, the guy picked up of the fifth ring and sounded out of breath. I gave my name and asked what he wanted.

"Hey, sorry, man. I was napping I guess," he said. Breathy voice, a little slurry.

"Who is this?" I asked.

"Speedy, ju know, from downtown?"

"You've got a phone now, Speedy?"

"Nah! It's the pay phone in front of Eddie's. Hey, I remembered something. Can you come down here?" I said sure, and we picked a place to meet up. I threw on a jacket and told Marti I was meeting a customer downtown. The '54 was blocking the garage, so I fired it up and *"chuff-clink,"* headed to town.

As I turned into the alley, I saw two people by the dumpster. Both looked ragged and dark in the distance. I pulled into the nice, new city parking and walked to the half-block alley. It appeared to be another bum, sorry, homeless person. Same green fatigue jacket and dirty jeans. He was maybe a little taller than Speedy, wearing a worn, knit ski cap. Speedy smiled as I got close. He seemed nervous about something. He said, "Hey," and I answered. So much for our tribal rituals.

"I think I saw something that might interest you?—you know? About that morning, you know?"

"Yeah? What did you see, Speedy?"

"Well, Diggs, here and I were making a 'can run' over to the recycler, you know."

"Yeah, over there?" I pointed in the recycler's direction.

"Yeah. Well, we usually go down Broadway and turn on D Street. because there's a bunch of little houses on Broadway, and we sometimes find cans in the alley behind. So we're pickin' cans out of the trash, see, and I see this car in a little garage there. And I remembered, see."

"You *remembered?*"

"Yeah. I remembered that car was in the back lot right next to the building." He pointed at my parked panel truck.

"That morning? You saw the car parked in lot the morning of the murder?"

"Yeah, but just for a little while. It must've been gone by the time you guys came. I didn't see it leave, but it passed me and Diggs when we was walking. I forgot because it was just there, and then it left."

"And where exactly were you?"

"I was in front of the dumper waiting for Billy. That's why I saw it. I was watching for Billy to come from that end of the alley."

"Okay. Let me understand it again now. You saw a car today that reminded you that you had seen it parked in the back lot that morning."

"Yeah!"

"And you saw it there while you were waiting for Billy to come from his squat."

"*Yeah!*"

"So Billy saw the car too?"

"Nah! He came around the front by the furniture store on Main. He surprised me." Speedy hooked a thumb over his shoulder, behind him, to the street end of the alley. There was a furniture store on the corner of the block, one of the only surviving stores on that downtown block. What they called an anchor.

"That was funny. He said he heard some people come in early, and he split. He went out the front door 'cuz it was open. He wanted to get away before they found his squat and him, so he bugged, and we went down the block like I said."

"So, Speedy, I thought you said before that you were waiting in back."

"Hey, you don't believe me?" His eyes lit up, and he backed a step and clenched his fists.

"No no, don't get excited. I'm just confused." I put my hands out. "Did I get it wrong?"

"Well, I…I just was having a little morning nip, you know." He nudged the bulge in his jacket. "You know? To get my head straight."

"Just a little nip."

"Yeah. I stashed the bottle under the dumpster that night, and I just stopped to top off on the way."

"Okay. Tell me about the car now."

"Oh, yeah, *the car*. Well, it was dark. One of those dark colors, or black or something. I didn't go close to it, but I remember it was dark. And it was one of those, uh, uh, it had a top that was, you know."

"Padded, a different color, what?"

"Nah! It was cloth, and it could go like—"

"It was a convertible? The top that folds down?"

"Yeah! A *con-ver-ti-ble*. Yeah, that's it. Hey, do you think you could spare any change, Vinnie?" I had anticipated this, and I handed him a twenty. He grabbed it with a flash of smile and turned to go.

"Speedy?" I spoke up as he walked away, anxious to put his new money toward his "heating bill." "Where was this house where you saw the car in the garage?"

"Oh, yeah." He and Diggs stumbled back toward me. "Well, it's on the third block, right near the corner of D Street. They don't have no numbers in the alley in back, but there's only a couple of garages right on the alley. Most of 'em have a little cement slab, but this is old and real small and made o' wood on the dirt. It's on the alley on the right side."

"Thanks, Speed."

He pocketed the bill, and he and Diggs trotted away, leaving the alley to its Saturday silence. I walked back to the truck, musing over the details. Speedy might still know something valuable if Bettencourt could tease it out of him. If he knew where to *find* Speedy, that is.

18

Hanging with My Homies

I cruised across town and turned down what I thought was the alley in question. There were several houses with garages. They all had them originally, but I guess many had been torn down. The houses had been built in the twenties for sure, frame and wood ship-lap siding, now with many, many coats of paint, *or not*. The garages that still stood were what I call Model A garages, just wide enough for an early Ford. I saw two that fit the description, and I wasn't sure what to do next. I tried calling the detective on my cellular, but he was off for the weekend. I didn't really want to leave a message; it would be too complicated. It was getting toward afternoon; there were Mexican kids all around, playing in the backyards behind the fences. The alley was half-blocked by a primered '65 Chevy Impala, the front end up on jack stands. The wheels hung down like broken arms. Three young men looked up as I got close. I shut the engine off and got out. *Chuff, click.*

"Hey, guys." I wasn't sure where to begin. Two of them had folded-handkerchief sweatbands on; the third had a red ball cap on backwards. All were wearing flannel shirts hanging loose, one top button closed. They had been kneeling by the front wheel, its tire lying against the fence. "You got brake trouble?" At least I knew something about brakes.

"Chu lost, my man?" Ball cap said, standing.

"Nah. I'm looking for someone."

"Well, chu found someone."

"Yeah, well, I'm looking for the house with a dark-colored convertible." That went over real well. They looked at me blankly. I was being too direct. "Hey, I had a friend tell me he'd seen the car parked around here." I went over to the wheel and squatted. "You gonna put on new shoes?" I tried again.

"What's it to chu, man?"

"I put '94 disk brakes on mine. *Really* stop well. Made a huge difference." I pointed to the '54 front end."

They turned to the panel for a minute and looked, evaluating the gray primered hulk.

"How you do that? Add-ons or you clip it?" This was one of the bandanas talking now.

"Yeah. Clipped the whole front end. Gave me better radiator mounts and hung the new motor and everything. Only thing I fabbed are the bumper brackets." They walked over to the truck, and I raised the hood. "Clipping" is the term for grafting the front of the frame of one car onto another. Alignment is critical, but it had made the changes on the old Chevy much easier. A package deal. Kind of like putting the top half of Arnold Schwarzenegger on my skinny body. *Woah! There's an image.*

"We have a lotta probs with the alignment and da ball joints on the Impala. That's what we were jawin' about. Hey, you're that painter guy?" This was said as they squatted down and looked underneath the fenders.

"That's me." I thought that Impala looked familiar. "Hey, I striped on this, didn't I? When d'ja prime it?"

"Bout a month ago. The trunk and the roof was getting rust spots bad."

"He don't gots a garage, and it sits out all the time." The other bandana put in.

"Well, *hey*. You wiped out my art, man." I smiled and he did too. "You gonna paint it soon?"

"I don't know, man. I got two kids, ju know? It might be a while."

"Only reason I can work on my old truck is that I don't have any. Sometimes I wish it was different, though." I smiled at him. "First things first, I guess."

"Yeah, I guess. So what's this stuff about a convert?"

"I just want to talk to them, but I don't see it around, and I don't know which house it is." I gestured at the two garages behind me.

"Ain't no one living in those houses, man." Red-hat speaking now. "They both for sale." The boys stood and walked back to the Impala. I guess the conversation was over. They seemed to forget me, so I drove the panel by them slowly, waved, exited the alley, made a left, and came around in front. They were right, of course. The two houses both had For Sale signs standing on the dry lawns and both of them saying, "Tribble Realty." I drove home thinking, *If you had to show a house, why park in the garage?*

The next morning, it wasn't until I was in the shower that I remembered that we were meeting the Grierson's at church. We talked about them as we got ready, and I tried to fill Marti in as we went. She asked me questions about Adele's house, how it was decorated and such. *What did that matter? Women!*

They were standing in front of the steps as we pulled into the lot beside the church. We greeted and introduced as we went inside. To my surprise, Bill saw several people he knew and waved at and shook hands with, and by the time we sat in a pew, I almost felt like *I* was the outsider.

Church was, well, church. It was a good Sunday, pastor all fired up on Hebrews 3. I thought that if the Griersons had any issues with Christianity, that ought to bring them out. Afterward, we stopped on the top step; and after more handshakes and greetings, we gave them directions to La Bamba. Marti was quiet in the car. "So what do you think?" I said, pulling out into the street.

"Adele says they were close to separating last year, but they're trying hard now to make it work."

"Just how did you find *that* out so fast?" *Women!*

"She complimented me on how dedicated you seemed to be. She saw you holding my hand. She wants Bill to be like you."

Oh, jeez. I thought over the lunch meeting and if I might have said something then. I couldn't remember anything specific. It's not that I mind being an example; *it was an honor.* But I couldn't remember doing anything so angelic that she would have been impressed with. I guess that's how it's supposed to be.

Luiz was doing the lunch duty and showed us to a table for four with a flourish of the menus. There were lots of couples either in preppy golf shirts and khakis chatting or in tennis shorts, caps, and sunglasses, reading the papers. *The members of the SMGC, the Sunday Morning Golf Club.* After we had ordered, several older couples wearing shiny suits and high-neck long dresses showed up. Church was out, and the conservative old guard shared the restaurant with the young rebels. I must have chuckled as I thought about it.

"What's so funny, Vinnie?" Bill smiled as he dug a chip in the salsa.

"Oh, just people, I guess. I was imagining what they were ordering." I gave an elbow point to the Four-Square foursome in the corner, next to some new professionals. "I'm guessing one beef enchilada with rice and beans for the suits and huevos rancheros for the college teachers."

"It *is* a town in transition, isn't it? In the Bay Area, people tend to do day trips. They all want to get away. Here in the valley, they all cluster." Bill looked thoughtfully.

"Well, that's just because there are so few really good places to go to. I bet a couple of 'boutique' restaurants could jump into the lineup and do well. Just look at Stockton."

"Yes, that's right, Vinnie. Once industry brings the young couples in, gives them trendy homes, they want somewhere stylish to go. It's all one big dynamic."

Our ladies were chatting up a storm. I looked at Bill and wondered where the conversation should go next, but the food came, and we smiled at the fragrant sauce and melted cheese. I spoke just as Bill reached for his fork. "Let's pray." I used the KISS principle, and then we began to eat. *Mr. Diplomatic.*

Bill finished first and sat back sipping his tea. "That was a nice prayer, Vinnie." *Another compliment. I'm really not used to this.*

"I don't know just how you mean that, Bill." *Maybe I could draw him out?*

"I'm used to more formal prayers, I guess. The church we went to before was very fixed in how they prayed. There were prayers for every occasion, but after a while, the big words got stuffy and old. Kind of lost their meaning."

"When I went to church as a kid, I memorized prayers like that. When I got older, I thought God might appreciate a more direct, conversational style. I just talk to Him now and don't even think about it."

"I wish I could do that." His voice had lowered, and I had to lean forward to hear it.

"What?"

"Just talk to Him. Things get so complicated sometimes." He stared at the artfully trimmed trees around the patio without really focusing on anything.

"When you know someone well enough, Bill, it's easy to talk to them. They're a friend."

"I never thought of God being a friend." He looked right at me now, his stare drilling through my face into my brain. "He's so, so *out* there."

"He can be, but he doesn't want to be. He wants to be our friend, at least that's how I understand Him."

"How does that happen—you becoming God's friend?"

"Just ask. Didn't Jesus say in Revelation, 'Behold I stand and knock. If *any* man opens, I will enter in and sup with him?'"

"Well, if you say so. I don't read the Bible much." He drank the last of his iced tea, and his ice clinked as he set the glass down.

"That's the beginning, Bill. Finding out for yourself just what He *does* say to you and then acting on it. What I or someone else says doesn't cut it. You need to take action for yourself." Conversation was getting a little strong for a lunch table. I wasn't hearing the girls in the background any more. "How about if I met with you a few times to get you started, say for breakfast? I think better in the morning."

"That might be interesting, Vinnie. If I just had time. These are busy weeks."

"I can get up pretty early, Bill, but it's up to you."

"Let me think about it. I'll call you."

"Sure. Well, ladies, all through?"

We smiled at one another and walked out after splitting up the bill. The Grierson's went one way and we went another. I wondered if Bill would even think about it at all. He was probably just being polite to the country boy. They seemed glad to go to church though. They had enjoyed it, but Bill was sure gun-shy about personal involvement. Marti said the same thing about Adele. She acted friendly to a point. She wanted to keep some things private.

19

A Nibble

The phone was ringing Monday when I unlocked the shop's front door. I missed it by the time I had shut off the hissing alarm, and I stared dumbly at the handset, willing it to ring again. But it didn't. I had a board on the easel in back, and after I started the coffee, I began to lay out the lettering with a Stabilo. I just about got it done when the ringing began again.

"Vinnie's," I answered.

"Hey, junior detective, how's it hanging?"

"Good, *Detective*. What's on your mind?"

"Well, I thought I should tell you we kicked Sorenson loose."

"Really?"

"Yeah, his lawyer was getting nasty, and all that we had was very circumstantial. Just the argument and those old fingerprints. I keep looking at it, but I don't see anything solid yet."

"I thought his prints—"

"Got the prints, but not the time. He claims he was there the day before, and he has a witness."

"Bummer! Uh, you need to talk to Billy again"

"What?"

"Talk to Billy again. He heard people come in the building before he left. He might know something more."

"Where'd this come from?"

"He's got a friend on the street. I don't think he'll talk to you, but this friend told me that Billy got scared out of his squat that morning by someone yelling."

"That's a good tip. I'll pull him in again."

"Can't you talk to him on the street? It would be *way* less threatening."

"Yeah, maybe I could."

"No tie, his turf, give 'em a Coke or a donut—something with sugar, that sorta thing?"

"Yeah. I'm working on that badge, Vinnie, thanks."

I had Turner's Body Shop call a little later. They had a striping repair, and I went over. It turned out to be a big deal, one whole side of a dually pickup. The truck had come from Fresno; you could tell from the striping style. That meant it was six or seven lines the whole length of the truck, one of them a half-an-inch-wide band. Just matching the five colors took me a half hour. It was a two-hour job, and it was after lunch before I got back to the shop. I saw the blinking light on the machine when I came in the door.

"Vincent. Bill Grierson. Can we meet Wednesday morning, maybe 6:00 a.m.? You said you got up early, Call me." He gave his cell number, and I scribbled it on the pad. His cell number, maybe we *were* getting somewhere. I called back, and we agreed to meet at a chain pancake place out near the freeway. It was a little less crowded than Eddie's. Their clientele was mostly truckers and travelers at that time of morning, and they had booths which would be more private. *That was exciting to hear.*

The only other phone call that afternoon was from CalNut Farms. They were a new partnership from back east that had bought out a local firm where I had previously done work. The secretary didn't sound too confident when she asked me to bid several signs that updated changes the new business wanted, placed probably at their plant entrances. It wasn't a big deal, but one that was important to the new owners. The plant had been a medium-big operation, accepting almonds and walnuts from local growers in addition to processing their own nuts. When I asked her about details (like what the sign would say and its size, *duh*) she grew flustered. She really wanted me to drive out there and measure the existing ones for myself. Gee, I really didn't want to do that, it being just a quote and all, and she sounded like she was just fishing for numbers anyhow. After spending some time finessing her, she agreed that their yardman could measure the signs, and she could phone me back. As I hung up, I wondered if I'd ever hear from her again.

20

Hard Words

And the evening and the morning were the next day, Wednesday. As I pulled into a spot at Pancake Heaven at oh-dark-thirty, I grew nervous. I had spent the time driving over, praying for a special awakening of the Spirit in me to best take advantage of Mr. Grierson's attitude. I thought about it and realized that this was, again, God's business and not mine. Now I relaxed. I went in and found him waiting in a booth with a coffee pot at the ready.

"Hey, Bill. Nice morning." I sat and filled my cup.

"Good morning, Vincent. Yes, it is." *Conversation is like a river. I needed to jump in and begin paddling.*

"So why are we here, Bill? How can I best serve you?" He looked down at the table and said nothing, and I was afraid I had already been too bold. Bill looked like a real "man's man." He was supposed to have had things all figured out. He wore his trademark ironed jeans and Cat construction boots. He had a dusting of grey in his blond hair. His eyes were the kind of blue that looks grey in some light, and their twinkle made me think that someone who risked such large sums of money would have to be pretty adventurous. I patiently sipped my coffee and waited. Finally, he looked up.

"Adele talks about this God-thing a lot, Vinnie. I think it's all well and good, but she seems to expect more of me than I know how to give. This is all new stuff. You've been married longer than I am. Maybe you can understand what I'm saying?"

"Can you be a little more specific about what you mean, Bill? I think I'm beginning to understand."

"Well, praying and all that is fine, and I don't even mind going to church. It's nice in its own way. The thing is she seems to *understand* it all, to get something out of it that remains a mystery to me. What is it? Is it a *woman* thing?"

"O.K. A lot of people think that going to church is like going to a service club, Bill. They go inside, they're friendly, they give a little money for a good cause, they listen to the speakers, and then they say goodbye and go to work." He nodded his head in agreement. "Worship is not like that, Bill. God didn't invent church. Church is something we invented. It's the current form of worship we use. Christians don't 'go to church' to meet together—that's incidental. They go to church to meet God, the Creator of the universe. I guess some people tag along, watch the service, and don't realize that He's *really there.* They don't talk to Him, don't listen for Him, and don't participate in it at all. Frankly, it sounds pretty dull to me. It's like being the third person on a date."

"What do you mean by 'worship' then?"

"Bill, I have to ask. How do you feel about scripture, about the Bible?"

"Well, it's a respected piece of literature. I don't pretend to understand some parts, but what I do understand is it's good. It is sensible."

"The Bible is God's wisdom about life written out inside. Sometimes, it's not written the way we talk today, but it's His message, all there for anyone to read. Here's the deal. God has said through the ages that man isn't, can't be good like Him. He's *Holy*, perfect. God is not just perfect (like: very nice, just what we wanted). He's p-e-r-f-e-c-t. He's in a whole different class. Do you understand that?" Bill was looking at his lap, not talking. I kept going. "He said that people could substitute animal sacrifice for their sins, their shortcoming, their un-perfectness, but that was in the past. God says that the blood of bulls and goats is not what he *really* wants, Bill. What He wants is obedience."

"That's pretty abrupt."

"Sacrifice was an important, really the *most* important part of Old Testament worship. God told Moses the way it was to be done.

He set the rules. What to do with the blood, what to do with the body parts, all that. But it's not what He ultimately wanted. The God of creation is not into BBQ."

"What is this 'obedience' then? To what? To His rules? Is that the Ten Commandments?"

"How do you feel if a sub does things differently than your plans ask for?"

"I make him rip it out. Plans are plans. They all know that."

"Do you know what God expects of us, individually?"

"Well, I try to do the best I can. How can He expect more than that?"

"God has many non-human attributes, Bill. God is not human. It's kind of hard to *get* some times. The most important way He is different than humans is that He is *holy*. He says to us in scripture, 'Be ye holy as I am holy.'"

"But we can't be like God. You already said that. So how can He expect us to be holy like Him?"

"The prophet Isaiah wrote, '*All* we like sheep have gone astray. We have turned everyone to his own way and the chastisement (the penalty) of our sins are upon Him.'" I sensed a little squirm in the pressed jeans. "Everyone tries to become holy *their way*, Bill. We know we aren't *holy*. We know it. People do things, hard things, and give up things and serve others. Some become very good. But Isaiah says that *no one* can become *holy* on their own. It's impossible. The apostle Paul says, 'there are *none* that do it right, no, not one.' It's like trying to reach a ten-foot ceiling with an eight-foot stud. It won't reach."

"So where does that leave mankind?"

"*Asking for help*. Isn't that the sensible thing to do? Jesus, God's son, says, 'I am the way, the truth and the light. No man cometh unto the Father but *by* me.'"

"So if I get this right, we go to church to worship Jesus, to thank Him for helping us, uh, you."

"Yes and no. Lots of folks think Jesus is fickle, Bill. He *won't* extend His help, His spirit, *to anyone* unless they *ask* for it. It's the ultimate respect thing. That's the core message in the New Testament.

Some people go to church and worship because they think Jesus will solve their problems automatically just because they're contrite. Now scripture does say clearly that He died for *all* of the world. But I think that means 'all' conceptually. I understand His help is available to all. But Jesus Himself says, 'Behold, I stand at the door and knock. If any one hears me and *invites* me inside I will come in to him and dwell with Him.' That's individually."

"Well, that gives me something to think about. I guess I wouldn't have much respect for a God that accepted people automatically. I can see how people are. A *real* God would have some kind of a selection process."

"He'll take anyone, Bill, if they are willing to come on *His* terms."

Bill looked down at his watch and said, "Hey! I've got to go. We'll do this again soon, okay?"

He got up, grabbed the paper check, and left. I sipped the last of my coffee and wondered if I had spelled it out right. There are so many people, and everyone sees the truth through a different lens of experience and prejudice. I was just myself, Vinnie the Brush.

21

Blessed Work

I was out of the shop most of Wednesday and Thursday doing trucks at a big dairy east of town. Every time I thought I was done, the owner would drive by where I was painting and add something else. It became almost funny. I guess he spent his days riding around in his pickup truck, traversing the dairy property, supervising his help. Like most of his milkers, by the end of the day, I began to work, looking over my shoulder. I lettered enough feed tanks and mailboxes for a lifetime that day. I'd be glad to finally get out of the wind. There were ominous clouds forming over the Coastal Range, and I wanted to go home. He gave up about 4:00 p.m., Thursday, and when I finished the last assigned line of copy, I headed home. It was going to take me a half hour to make sense out of my notes in order to make out the bill. I had it scribbled all over the work order, and I had used up every open space and margin on the page with all his additions. So, anyway, my mind was occupied as I parked behind the shop.

A call from the CalNut secretary was on the machine. The secretary had figured it all out and wanted to talk, and I called her back. She had indeed gotten all the info together, and it was easy to give her a bid. She said the price was fine (a pleasant surprise), and she would give it to her boss to be "*blessed.*" That was a new one for me, but not a bad use of the term. I washed up the stuff from the dairy job and re-oiled the brushes in my kit for the truck. I was refilling the black paint bottle for the kit when the phone rang.

"Vincent?" It was Bill's business-like voice. I was getting used to recognizing it.

"Hey, Bill. What's going on?"

"Fine, Vincent. Uh, I have thought over what you said at breakfast the other day, and I wondered if we might meet again?"

"Sure, Bill. When and where?"

"Would tomorrow be too soon? I realize that it's short notice."

"That's fine. Same place?"

He agreed and hung up. I prayed for guidance as I finished filling my kit's paint bottles. He seemed to have decided something, and I wondered what it was.

The phone rang again, and it was Car-Renu Collision Body Shop. They wanted to bring over a flatbed truck from the local lumberyard that had been repaired. I hung up and went out back to clear a space to put it. I was just putting the paint back in my truck when I heard it coming down the street. I moved the sawhorses and hoped it would fit. Some of these older flatbeds are pretty long. The companies usually bought a bare cab and frame, and had someone local build the bed. Sometimes, they got a little too creative. I guided it in, and the tail *just* cleared the door swing. The driver's door was clean and white, and looked like it belonged somewhere else, on some other truck, since the rest of it was filthy. I was closing the barn door as the Mexican boy from the body shop hopped down and walked out saying I should fix it up like the other side. I would deal with it tomorrow.

Marti was home when I got there. She was tending her flowers in the back yard. I got a soda from the fridge and went outside.

"How's it goin', hon?"

"I just wanted to get some of these weeds out before dinner."

I squatted down behind her. "You have a good day?" I took a long drink and felt the bubbles burn the back of my throat, and watched Marti's face wrinkle in the sunlight.

"Yeah, I guess. Myrna's in a tantrum again. She ordered another wrong shade of roses for a wedding tomorrow, but we can't swap these this time. I think it'll work, but she is pretty hard to talk to right now, so I snuck out early."

"I heard from Bill again. We're going to meet tomorrow morning."

"That's *good*. Is he interested in the Lord?"

"I don't know, really, but I figure the Lord's interested in him."

22

Pancake Presentation

Friday, glorious Friday. The pancake shop was a little fuller this morning, all the two-wheeler weekend warriors fueling up for the road. The parking slots just in front of the doors were stuffed with Harleys and the Can-Am wannabes. It was a pretty nice day, and the rain clouds had slid by us without ill effect. I guess the biker boys were going out for a tour of the foothills. Bill wasn't here yet, and I got to the coffee first. I sat there, fresh cup warming my hands while I surveyed the ambiance and tried to make an intelligible prayer to compose my jumbled thoughts. Sometimes, you have to just go with the flow that's set in place. I saw Bill through the front doors; he seemed his usual purposeful self. He shoved the door open, walked into the lobby, and looked around until he saw me.

"Sorry I'm late, Vinnie." I made a gesture with my hands and slurped some more coffee down. He poured himself a cup and sipped. "I don't know where to start."

"Start wherever you need to, Bill."

"I have a problem that's very personal. I don't know how to solve it. and it's in the way of any commitment I could make with God."

"Bill, there could not be *anything* or condition that could keep you from God." He started to protest and I stopped him with my raised hand. "Let me finish, and I know I'm a little out of line here, so give me some slack. God knows all about you and your life. He knows your plans. He knows your sins. He knows your dreams. He knows your shortcomings. In the Bible, He says that He loves us in spite and *because* of these. The only thing that He allows to keep us from Him is our sin, and Jesus's sacrifice erased the power of that. We just have to accept it, Him, like a gift you unwrap. We can't *do* anything to clear the way, it's there, offered free and clear. God just wants us to surrender. You have to realize that He says in the Bible over and over that *He* has plans for us too, and *His* plans are greater and better and more appropriate for us than we could ever imagine. He probably has your problem's solution all ready. We think we're giving up everything when we surrender to Him—we're not. Well, we are, but He gives us, in return, more than we ever dreamed." I stopped talking. I get on the subject and I start to preach, and I didn't want to preach right now. Not to an audience of one.

He was quiet for a while, and he sighed twice. I had blown it; I was sure. Then he asked, "So what do I do?"

I grinned. I couldn't help myself. "You just ask Him in. You open your heart up and let Him in. Some people think it takes a speech, some special formula of words like those big-word prayers you talked about, but it really only takes your mental bowing. Usually, it's done in a prayer. Look, here's what I prayed: 'God, I'm a sinner, and I have no right to ask except for Your Son's sacrifice for me. I ask to be adopted into Your family based on Jesus's death on the cross. I ask that Your Holy Spirit come into me and change me so that I might be acceptable to You.'"

"Okay, and then what?"

"And then, Bill, fasten your seat belt because the ride's gonna begin."

23

How to Lose a Badge

For a Friday, it was exceedingly slow. The phone didn't ring, no one came by, and I just painted away. In a way, it was discouraging because I was really pumped from my talk with Bill. But there was no one to share it with. It wasn't a thing I should call Marti about; I would tell her when I got home. I called Mooney, down in Palmeria. Mooney is a buddy that does the same thing I do, except he does more striping and I do more signs. Mooney and I share quite often via Ma Bell. I had met Mooney and his wife at a Letterhead meet years ago. I put my headset on now and dialed the phone.

"Moon's Lines and Signs."

"What are *you* working on, on a Friday?"

"Hello, my friend. I'm finishing a big ol' black suburban. You know, something different." Mooney striped a suburban at least once a week, and most of them they sent him were black. Nice to have an 'in' with a local Chevy dealer.

"What're *you* doin'?"

"Oh, I'm just lettering some boards, but that's not why I called. Something neat happened."

"What?"

"Well, I told you about that contractor and his wife that came to church?"

"Yeah."

"Well, we've met for coffee a couple of times and this morning, he accepted Christ."

"*Good-o.* How did it go?"

"He had some questions, and then we prayed, right there in the middle of Pancake Heaven. Is that cool, or what?"

"Yezza, Yezza. That be total coolness. You know, it's been a long time since I prayed with anyone. A long time."

"It has for me too. I kinda feel we ought to be doing it more, Moons."

"I agree. Say, not be mundane, but what's going on with the murder?"

"Well, Harley is looking into some things. But all of the suspects have fallen through so far. I don't know what to think. *Somebody* did it."

"That's too bad. Tough to think somebody could get away with a thing like that. Hey, I got to go. The driver is coming for this sub soon, and it better be finished."

"Okay, bro. See ya."

I had lied, not realizing it at the time. I had an idea on the case to pursue, and it was sitting in my desk drawer. I did a little more lettering, and then I finally called Harley, gritting my teeth.

Boy, was he mad! His car came zooming down the street a few minutes later, hooked a youie right into my curb. He slammed the door on the squad and while it was still rocking, stomped through the shop into the back room. I almost turned the air conditioner on to abate the steam he was giving off. You think I'm being funny. I'm not.

"*Do you have any idea what you've done? Vincent, the first twenty-four* hours are the *prime* time for an investigation. After that, we have to dig through the lies and fabrications that the murderer has since created. *Now* you come up with important evidence? *Now?* Two weeks later?" he huffed and puffed around the shop while I got the key ring out of my drawer. I held it out to him, hoping to soften his attitude, but he screamed, "*Put...that...down!*" So I dropped it on the counter.

He went back into the shop, tore off a piece of paper towel, and returned to gingerly wrap the keys up. "I suppose it was too much for me to expect that you would be careful of the forensics! I suppose you just picked them up at the scene?"

Finally, he paused his shouting, and I could see he was trying to cool himself down. Maybe he was waiting for me to say something. I tried to be clear in what I did say. "I kicked them across the floor as I was looking for Clare. It was dark. I thought they had fallen out of my own pocket. I picked them up and pocketed them because I thought they were my keys at the time. When I found the body, I totally forgot about them. When I got back to the shop, I pulled them out of my pocket, but of course, they wouldn't open my lock, and I realized I had another set of keys. In the excitement, I tossed them in my drawer and completely forgot until now. Geeze, Harley, I didn't plan to do this, *really*."

He was writing in his little notebook, scribbling as fast as he could. He muttered something about civilians and forensics, and then he grabbed the towel-wrapped keys and walked briskly out of the shop without so much as another word, leaving me just the jingling of the bell and the slam of the door.

❧

"So that was my Friday, how was yours?" The buzz of the restaurant didn't make me feel any better. Marti had agreed to meet me at Pasta! Pasta! after work. She looked like I felt, tired and ready for a rest day. (Course she had to work half day this Saturday, but it would be light duty.)

"Well, not as wild as yours." She smiled through her iced tea. "That's great news about Mr. Grierson. I know Adele has been so worried about their marriage. She really loves Bill. Lately, she says that he seems so preoccupied. She's afraid he's thinking of leaving her. This decision, this change has got to help."

"Only time will tell, babe."

She reached across the linen and grabbed my hand. "Funny how we all have ups and then downs, isn't it?" *My girl always got the last word.*

24

How Not to Tell People

The phone rang Saturday morning. Marti was just leaving for work, so I answered, but handed it to her as soon as I heard who it was. Marti talked just a little and hung up.

"That was Adele. She wants us to come for lunch tomorrow. I told her we'd be delighted." She smiled and trotted out to the garage. What was that about?

I was hoping to hear from Harley, but I knew it wouldn't happen. I also knew I'd better be real quiet around him until he got over my mistake. I mean, I didn't try to pick up stuff at the scene. It just fell in my way. I guess I could have been a little more careful. But Jezz, it *was* my first murder scene, and I really didn't know what to look out for anyway.

I mowed the lawn and cleaned up the yard, and after a quick sandwich, I went out to the garage to work on the truck. *I'm glad I didn't sign Ephesians 2:10 to this one.*

I had bought a satellite radio unit and decided to do the install. It was harder than I expected—the special antenna and all. Not difficult, just different than I had done before. I try to keep up with new stuff, but things are getting so different, so unique, that I wonder about the future of DIY projects. It seems like you need some special education before you can do most stuff these days. I mean, it's not connecting wires; it's all these new connectors and special crimps and plugs. Things keep getting all specialized and complicated from the last time I did it. By about four thirty, I got the antenna connected to the radio, and I turned it on.

Suddenly, everything in the world was fine. I had some 120 special stations to choose from, and the digital dial readout gave me information on each choice so that picking out the stations was actually fun. I realized that a lot of life is like that for me. Events seem so difficult, so impossible; and then when you try to put it together, everybody requires different treatment—specialized treatment. Get the relationships right and it all clears up, and things seem to work like a well-engineered machine like they are supposed to. *Supposed to*. Kinda like there is someone who designed this whole thing, right?

Sunday was just fine. Pastor was in fine fiddle again (whatever that means), and we motored over to the Grierson's house afterward. If they were in attendance, we hadn't seen them at church. There was a tired and plain-Jane Ford Vicky parked in the driveway that I didn't recognize. Maybe their grandma was visiting. Marti hadn't been to the house before, and she was in awe of the little extras on the outside. The porch trim details and the brickwork on the walk leading up to the door (which, I have to admit, I had not noticed). *If you have the money*, well it was very nice. She was pointing out the features as the door opened, and Bill beckoned us inside, sporting a wide smile. The conversation was filled with "how did you do this" and "I love that" as we passed through the family room and out onto the covered patio.

Marti was almost shocked to get a big hug from of all people, Ginnie Soares. I was surprised to see the secretary at this intimate lunch. Bill grinning, introduced her, but Marti and I both knew who she was. Or thought we knew. We just didn't know why she was there. Bill then said she was the fiancée of his brother, Brad (who was busy grilling something at the barbeque.) Brad gave us a wave as he moved pieces of our future lunch from place to place on the grill and then onto a platter.

We stood with glasses of iced tea, chatting with the folks. I watched Brad clean up the grill. He was rather meticulous and scraped and then brushed the grill down before he shut it off and closed the lid. Lugging a full platter of skewers of meat to the table, he appeared to be nonchalant. His eyes were smallish but looking everywhere at once as if taking visual notes, kinda feral-like. Wearing a lime knit shirt over slim tan jeans, he looked neat, but something didn't quite fit. No cowboy-cool here. I held my tongue. I realized that Bill had a lime shirt too, and then I saw the embroidered GH logo on the heart space.

Adele carried out a large bowl of greens, and Ginnie followed with corn ears stacked high on another serving platter. Marti made girly sounds under her breath like it was a fashion show or something. She was all about presentation. I just salivated and knew a feast when I saw one.

Adele cleared her throat and elbowed Bill who turned to me and asked if I would pray for the meal. We were standing around the table, so it seemed natural. I bowed and made a brief thanks for the food, and I noticed Brad's expression as I raised my eyes. It was a peculiar expression. I can't really say contempt; it was subtle and yet "in my face." It sure wasn't happiness. I guessed that he had reservations about something.

We sat down, but I heard him ask Bill if this was something to do with their earlier conversation. Bill waved him quiet, and we dug in to the food. Which was great, I might add. Adele had done something to the meat that was really tasty. I finally got it out of her; that it was lamb marinated in some sauce. Boy, she had left the Bimboville city limits *way* behind as far as I was concerned.

Conversation covered the town and all the things that new people want to know, and I let Marti give her opinions right and left. Why this street is called, who decided that, and so on. We were done eating way too soon. The women cleared the table, and I took a cup of coffee to nurse.

The brothers displayed an odd chemistry. Bill was the boss, but Brad was quite free with his criticism and direction. It didn't seem to bother Bill. I just watched, trying to figure it all out. I thought Bill was cool; he gave in to his brother from time to time. It looked like a good leadership style to me.

I have a brother and a sister, but they live far away, and I don't get to do much more than talk to them on the phone a few times a year. We live pretty separate lives. One thing though, I don't ever remember either of them telling me what to do with my business. Ah, the joys of siblinghood.

Finally, Bill paused and said, "Wait a minute, Brad. You don't understand it yet. I gave up control of my life to God this week. You can call me a Christian, or something else if you like. You can call me *crazy* if it makes you happy. Things are going to change at work. I'm sorry, but they have to. There's no danger to you, Brad." He laid a hand on his brother's shoulder. "Don't fight me. It's not a bad thing. Get used to a new brother, and I hope a much better one. Just give me a while to work things out."

Well, I guess I won't be embarrassed about a little thing like my praying anymore. That speech was like a glove thrown down between them. Brad turned away, and I had to say something. *Vinnie the mouth.* "Wait a minute, Brad. I know we've only just met, but I don't understand what the problem is. Can you explain it to me, or is this something private with your brother?"

"It's something a little of both, Vincent. *Little* brother here has decided to change the direction we run our business. Or maybe I should say *his* business because *I'm* not going to be a part of it."

He stamped up the steps into the house and shouted, "Come on, Ginnie!" and out of the house they went, her high heels clipping on the cement, trying to keep up with his stomping boots.

"Well, Vincent, that wasn't what I intended. Not at all." Bill looked down at his lap and sighed. I wasn't sure what to say. With the slam of the front door, the table seemed suddenly empty.

"What did you tell him, Bill?" *Vinnie the peacemaker.* Adele came out and refreshed their teas, and then she and Marti sat quietly back down.

"I told Brad that I had invited God into my life and that there might be some changes in the company because of it. That's all. I told him I would let him know what I was thinking before I did anything. That was it. I had no idea he would blow up over what I said. All I was thinking about was tithing, really. What did I do so wrong?"

Marti smiled and answered, "You didn't do anything wrong, Bill." She reached over and squeezed his hand on the tabletop. "It's Brad, not you. Many people think that life with Jesus will be sweet and smooth." I felt her other hand walk back over my thigh and grab my hand, too. "We can tell you that's not an accurate assessment." She was doing well, so I kept my mouth closed. (*Vinnie the politician.*) She continued, "Sometimes, the Spirit of God moves in people far differently than we expect. Our job is to hang on and accept the changes as He makes them."

"I just don't get what Brad is so worked up about. We've made money together. He paid off his new house here with Grierson money. Do you think he—"

"There's no telling what he thought, Bill," I cut in finally. "He might have expected that you were going to quit and become a minister or a missionary. Some people can't see that regular Christians just live. They think if you change, that you are becoming, to them, a radical going off starting some flamboyant behavior. I think that's what's going on in his head, but I think there's something more too. I sensed something else, some personal concern. Do you know what it could be?"

"Not a clue. Brad has been busy on all the contract stuff since we got here. He was setting up relationships with the contractors and the real estate guys. Just all the prelim arrangements we needed to go through. The only other thing in his life I know about was his falling for Ginnie. She's such a sweet gal and a good match for him. I really hoped things would work out better for us as a family."

25

Homie Vinnie

On my way to work the next day, I decided that another talk with my favorite detective was finally appropriate. I had to smooth things out with him somehow. Take my lumps. So I called him and left a message on his voice mail. Always the hard worker, I'd expected to have to leave him a message.

I had an unexpected visitor at the shop that morning. The dude with the red ball cap from the alley came in just after I opened up. He introduced himself this time. His name was Hildago, Hilly to his friends on the street.

"Hey, mon. I was tinkin' after chu left last week. Whachu tink about doin' sometin' on the primer on my 'pala?"

"If it's gonna be painted like that for a while, then it works for me. What you got to put down, my man? You don't mean *do it gratis,* do you?"

"Oh, heck no, bro. I could give you maybe one large, maybe? Chu could do somethin' simple but nice?"

"You can spare the green? I don't want to be robbing any little kids now?" I hoped I wasn't being too silly, using the street patois. I was trying to see it from his point of view.

"Nah. The old lady and I miss the lines on the sides. She says it's like car jewelry. Without it, the ride looks nekid. She kept some back from the house money, and I had a good week at work. It's okay."

"So when you want to do it?"

"Well, dats the thing, homs. I got the front end all tore up just now. We putting new ball joints and new brakes on it. It's in the back yard up on blocks. Could you do it there?"

Now this is not an unusual situation at all. Guys figure since the car is in one place, disabled as it were, that I can work on it while it sits. And I can. "When, Hilly?"

"Hey, anytime this week. I'm tryin' to get it done for this week-end. There's a show in Fresno we wan' to hit. Be cool if it were decked out by then. Chu come over in the day, and my wife, she watch you. Maybe get you a cold one, you know?"

"You'd trust me, would you?" He could see I was pulling on him now, kidding.

"Hey, if you workin' on my ride, I trust you with my kids."

"All right, can't miss out on that kind of a deal. I'll be over tomorrow."

26

Striping and Entering

So the next morning, I rolled down the dirt alley and pulled up at Hilly's back gate. Monday had been pretty quiet. This morning, Hilly's pretty wife was hanging clothes on the wires in the back yard next to the Impala. I saw that Hilly had reprimed the '72 body with gray but had shot the roof with white primer. It made a nice contrast; kind of what the guys call the Bellflower look.

I suppose I need to explain that. In the late fifties and sixties, cruising the drive-ins in the LA West Valley was the thing to do on the weekend. A style of car developed around the little suburb of Bellflower. It favored long chrome exhaust tubes out under the back fender edges, white painted top, wire wheels, and lacey striping, all comprising the "look." Kinda an early "low rider" thing. Hilly was getting there. He didn't have much money, but he did have a thing for style.

I opened the gate and "hola-ed" at the wife. I had my kit and a low stool in hand, so I think she figured out who I was. I walked around the car, wiped the areas off with cleaner, and laid some guide tape down. After a few quick wide lines for the theme, I striped the thin accents. I tried not to get carried away, but on a big clean car like an Impala, it's hard not to. It was a large canvas. I was outside where things dried rapidly, so I had to move fast. Blues and dark gray swirlies on the gray primer and a few light gray lines on the white should pull it all together.

I was pretty much done by noon. I knocked on the back door and told the missus that I would be back after I got a burrito at the trucks. I still had a little cleaning up to do. I repacked my kit and stowed it in the back of the pickup. I didn't see anyone around, so I crossed the alley and walked carefully around those two little garages. There weren't any windows, but there were cracks in the wood doors. One side was obviously out of use, filled with boxes and broken furniture. The other was empty but with tire prints on the dirt floor. I could see someone had been in and out of the dirt entrance, but the space was empty now. Pretty distinct tire marks though.

I rolled over to the taco truck and ordered and stood aside like I was big and tough. When I heard, "Torta de jamon," I strolled to the window and held out my five. I got the requisite one and a quarter and a dime, and a nickel. Hey, why argue? It's only money. Can't we all just get along?

It was a good ham sandwich, but I had to discard just a few of the green pickled jalapenos. I'm too gringo to buy into that thing. I talked with a couple of guys who were eating there from one of the body shops nearby. Then my cell rang.

"It's about time." I had seen the number on the cell readout.

"So what's up?" I could hear Harley was still being reserved.

"Harley, I know it's a lot to ask, but do you think you could bring those keys and meet me somewhere?"

"They're locked up in evidence, Vincent."

"Yeah, but I think I figured something out. Come on, *Detective*. I'm on your side. You won't need a warrant. You're not going inside."

"I guess so, but I have to bring someone with me then for chain of evidence purposes."

"In the alley between D and F off Broadway, you'll see my pickup."

I went back, wiped down the Imp, and signed my tag on the trunk edge. I was, of course, hoping for a little advertisement. I had done more work than he was paying for, but that was on me. The car just needed it. I got my camera and shot a few pics for the book. The señora stepped to the door and called me over. She offered me a wad of twenties and said, "Gracias," and smiled demurely. I pocketed it without counting and said, "De nada," and I went out to the truck to wait. It would have been impolite to count the wad in front of her. In front of her husband, it would have been different; but really, these were not people that would cheat me.

The cops weren't long in coming. At least they had still taken me seriously. I stepped up to the passenger door as the unmarked rolled up behind my truck. It's kind of funny to call it an unmarked. Who else would drive a white four-door sedan with black wheels and multiple trunk antennas? I told Harley what I had in mind and about the convertible Hilly had seen parking in the skinny garage. They followed me across the alley and looked in the garages through the cracks. Then they trooped through the yard to the back door of the first house. Harley pulled the keys out of their plastic bag and tried them in the door. None of the four did any good. I smiled in embarrassment and did a soft shoe dance on the weedy back lawn to detract from my shrinking cred.

Harley led his partner across the lawn to the similar house next door. Harley still wasn't happy. He had on his steely face that made me nervous. First, I had withheld evidence, and then I jerk his chain on this. I had hoped that this would refresh our budding friendship. Maybe I had inadvertently sprayed it with round up. He tried the keys again. The first three wouldn't go in, but the fourth opened the screen door.

Harley waved me aside and both of the policemen stepped into the back porch. There was another locked door and Harley tried the keys, and another one fit that lock. I waited while they disappeared inside and then came back out. Harley was fighting back a small smile as he headed to the car.

"I thought if you didn't have a warrant, you couldn't go inside?" I was stumbling across the abandoned lawn, trying to catch up.

"I got a provisional warrant that lets us enter *if* the keys fit, Vincent."

"So did you see anything?"

"Not now, Vincent," was his only reply. I didn't think that was very nice. After all we'd done together. Here I am, practically solving the crime for them, and he wouldn't share. I just wanted to know. I didn't really want the badge thing. I thought about picking up my marbles and not playing anymore. *Mu, mu, mu.*

We trooped back to the unit while the other officer sat down on the porch steps and wrote in a pocket notebook. Harley had a mumbled conversation on the radio in cop shorthand. I couldn't make it out. Finally, he waved me closer.

"Vincent, I want you to go on back to your shop. I have things to do now, and they have to be done correctly. I can't have a *civilian* in the *way* right now."

A *civilian?* What did he think this was? He looked at me, and since I couldn't break his stare, I relented and got in the truck. I felt somehow abandoned, yet as I drove away, I realized that I was the one leaving.

During my second cup of coffee back at the shop (and I didn't gulp this one), I began to simmer down a scoche. The physical act of brush lettering kept me occupied while my brain tried to work things out. I got a *lot* of lettering done that afternoon.

I have a friend who says, "God's will isn't democratic." It took me a while to understand what he meant when he said that. Simply stated, it means that God's will is just that—*God's* will. Our opinions don't change it or make it happen sooner or later. We're not a part of the process; we're not a jury. God's will just "is." We have our supposed understandings, but He is what He is. *We* need to adjust to Him. *He's* the one driving the bus. If this was *His* will, then I needed to accept it, and my part in it.

I was hoping for an investigatory role in the case. But I wasn't an investigator; I wasn't even a detective. Heck, I'm not sure I was really even a witness. Actually what I was, was a bystander, and it didn't really matter what I wanted. This was how it was working out. I could hear the small gentle voice of the Spirit saying, *"Get with the program, Vincent."*

I liked Harley. He could be hard-nosed about his work, but he was an all-right guy. I thought more about it. I dug out a piece of redwood I had been saving for a special project. I sanded the face off, gave it a coat of varnish, and set it to dry.

The phone rang just as I was leaving for the day. "Vincent, it's Bill."

"Hey, Bill! What can I do for you?" There was some kind of noise in the background. He was speaking loudly to make himself heard.

"Can you come down to the jail, Vincent? I've been arrested."

27

Jailhouse Ministries

I sat in the interview room waiting for Bill to be brought from the holding cells. I had called Marti, and she had gone over to be with Adele. Driving over to the jail, I had time to chew over the details. Normally, RPD wouldn't let an arrestee have a visitor yet, but Harley had decided to work his magic. Maybe his anger *had* cooled. Harley would have to sit in, of course, but that was all right.

Why Bill had been arrested at all was a complete mystery to me. If he had done something, sure, that would make sense. But in my head, it just didn't work. I knew that Harley must have some evidence, but what? There sure wasn't any clear motive for Bill to mess up all of his new prospects in the valley by killing someone, and Bill wasn't an impulsive person. I remembered the slashy, ragged character of the wounds. I was expecting it to be someone with anger inside. Bill was full of regret. *His brother now.* I parked and went inside.

There was noise in the hall, and the door opened. Bill came in, resigned but normal otherwise. No cuffs, just arms at his sides, resigned. Harley directed him to sit opposite me at the table. Bill didn't smile, but he wasn't sad-looking, just subdued. Harley remained standing. He slapped his file on the table and flipped it open.

"Need to go over a few things, Mr. Grierson. Tell us (*ou-o-o, us*) about this knife set you have." *What?*

"Well, I was given it as a gift. Well, my wife was, actually."

"By who?"

"By my brother, Brad, last Christmas. What has this to do—"

"Just answer the questions, Mr. Grierson. I understand one is missing from your set." *Not a question.*

"Yes, yes."

"How long has it been missing?"

"Well, just about two, three weeks. I'm not sure. We didn't notice it until just the other day. We don't use that set much. We thought that in our moving, it had been misplaced."

"Who noticed it first?"

"I did. I asked Adele about it, and she said it was probably misplaced during the move, she thought. You don't think that *that* is the knife. Oh, my." Now the silence was thick enough to cut with…

"Did you know Clare Tribble?"

"Yes, we had a tentative business relationship."

"Please explain."

Bill looked at the ceiling and leaned back. "Well, when we first looked for a place in the valley, we talked to the local realtors, and I met Clare that way. He had ideas and had some interesting land parcels under contract. We talked about development property, how the business market was going over here." Bill went spacy like he does and stared at the ceiling for a minute. "Actually, Clare is the reason we moved to Riverglen. He invited Adele and I to look around the area, and we just liked what we saw."

"Who exactly is *we*? Your wife and you?"

"Well, no. The company, Grierson Brothers Construction."

Harley flipped his note pages. "I thought the title was Grierson Construction. I don't remember 'brothers' being in it."

"Yeah, Brad changed that. He thought it sounded better without the 'brothers' in it, sounded more contemporary."

"And that office building? How did you get involved with that particular property?"

"Clare found it. He knew about it, I guess. He set the deal up with the owner, and we were about to get it into escrow."

"Did you have a key to the building?"

"Yes! We'd just been given a key from Clare, so we could measure and plan the remodel. Brad was supposed to give it to my head guy, Dave Santos. He was going, *is* going, to do the remodeling."

"Who has that key now? Where is it?"

"Let me think. I *think* it's with Brad. He's the point man on the remodel, but I really don't know."

"Vincent, do you want to ask anything?" *Whoa, Harley was being awfully generous.*

I leaned forward. Bill was still cool and under control. I just couldn't see him doing this stuff, but if he had access to the key and the knife was his. "Bill, who actually owns the building right now? You're not in escrow yet. Is it still a Marchant family property?"

"Well, you know how things get tangled up, Vincent. I'm not sure who actually holds the title right now. The Marchants must have sold it because the owner is supposed to be some LLC in the Bay area. I think the name is SG LLC. I was kind of surprised at that. They're some corporation. Wish we could have gotten it from the Marchants directly. It would probably have saved us some money."

"Harley, are we done here, for now?"

"Yes, if you are through you'll have to leave. I've got some phone calls to make."

"Can I pray with Bill before he goes back?"

I don't think Harley got that request very often. Or maybe he did. He didn't know how to answer. Finally, he spread his hands, sighed, and nodded. We prayed, and Bill got another lesson in Contemporary Christian Life 101. I just didn't see that he could be duplistic or guilty. "Bill, keep your seat belt tight," I said. "This ride isn't over yet."

A uniformed officer took Bill back to a cell, and I turned to Harley when we were alone again. "I know I'm not an official part of this, Ratty. I appreciate you letting me talk to Bill."

He looked around and hissed, "I *told* you I don't use that name any more."

Holding back my laugh I said, "Well, I appreciate your kindness anyway. What are you going to do next?"

"Check the papers we find in Clare's office, verify what Bill told us. No one to ask at the office anymore, we just have to follow the facts we can find."

I thought a minute. "Hey, what about Ginnie, his secretary? She works for DelMac now." Harley smiled, nodded, and wrote in his notebook. "Always good to know these little tidbits, Vincent."

"I'll see you then." I checked my watch. "I've got to get home. Say, aren't you about through for the day?"

He gave a slight grin and kept writing. "The law never sleeps, Vincent."

28

Research

Marti wasn't home, and I called her on her cell to see what we were doing about supper. She suggested we meet at a local Chinese fast food place. She said Adele would come too. So when we did I was able to bring Adele up to speed, as they say.

Adele was as bewildered as I as to why the police had arrested her husband. Harley wouldn't tell me, but he had just said that they had good reason. Bill wasn't exactly charged, and he still could have called a lawyer, but he wanted to wait and give the police time to see that he was innocent. He said his life was in the Father's hands. This might be a kind of naive way to deal with the law. Frankly, I was amazed to see such a new Christian with so much trust in God's protection. He was right, but I was amazed at how mature his newfound faith had grown.

Adele did mention that the police had used a search warrant to take her knife set from their kitchen. They had had an item-specific search warrant. That sounded like pretty clearly directed suspicions. I asked her about the loss of the knife and who knew about it, and she was immediately bewildered. No one in town knew they owned the knives. They hadn't had many visitors. We talked about Bill and Adele's life together, and I mentioned the distinct change in Bill's demeanor. Finally, we talked about the brother. Adele voiced some mild concerns. Brad had been very positive about what he was finding out about conditions until just recently. Adele said that Bill was worried that the two brothers were beginning to disagree quite a bit. I thought about the changes to my sign drawings (*selfish Vinnie*). I guess Bill was right.

She said that nothing about the planned office had been clearly decided yet. I asked her what she meant by that. She said that the cost of the building had changed. Clare had negotiated a fair price that left the Griersons room in their budget to develop and decorate. But when Del got to the final papers, the price had strangely jumped one hundred thousand. Brad had told Adele that it was unavoidable, that the seller had changed their mind.

We finished the food and the fortune cookies, mine being that I was going on a short vacation. Marti took Adele back to her house. Once back home, I sat with Marti and reviewed what we knew. I needed to find out the true ownership of the building. It was too late to call anyone, but I tried some web searching on the home computer. I found that the Marchants had indeed sold the offices to SG LLC. No mention of price details, just a date of the paper change. I tried to find who that SG was, but it just wasn't possible with what was posted on the county websites. I thought about Del, and that maybe he could look up legal stuff through realty channels, but of course, he was in the middle of it and might not want to. I thought that talking to Harley was not a good idea just now.

The next morning, I went to Eddie's for breakfast where it all began for me. Like clockwork, Del came in. I got him to sit next to me and asked him about a search. He said he didn't really need to. He said that SG LLC was only a post office box in the Bay area. He had never been able to meet with them physically. He had thought about searching it further on his own but just hadn't done it. He smiled and said he'd do some more looking around this morning.

I had a customer with a new blank van waiting when I got to the shop. It was an all-day job, one I had done on another of their company vehicles, so I dug out the patterns from the last job. My brain was on autopilot until the afternoon. Not Just Another Carpet Cleaner, clever name, that. The job went quickly. I began to wonder why I hadn't heard from Del or Harley. Harley didn't answer his phone, and Del was out of the office, so I got back to work and had finished up the truck by three. After that, I was stuck with time on my hands. People who picked up work were usually late, and I didn't realistically expect the truck owner to show up until after four.

So I took a chance and did a quick drive over to DelMac's office. The purple Mustang was there, and I saw Ginnie through the front door. When I came in, she smiled and said hello. I asked about Del, and she said that he had left several hours ago. I pushed, and she said he was meeting with a client. I tried to get the name out of her, but she just wouldn't tell me. *Great.* I turned to leave, and she asked me what the rush was. I said that Del was looking into something for me. I didn't want to say more and she didn't have anything else to say, so I left and went back to the shop.

The van owner was waiting for me when I returned. Amazingly, he was on time. He was a little huffy about my not having been there. *You can't please everyone.* He signed the bill, thanked me, and took the van. I guess I was supposed to wait on the money. I was just about to lock up when the phone rang. It was Brad Grierson. *There's a surprise.* He wanted me to drop by his house.

29

My Other Brother

The Hedberg house had always been a local historical site. The town had been settled by several families, and the Hedbergs were one of the most successful. Perhaps I should note: *burg* is Swedish and *berg* is Danish, or German. Around here, we learn that stuff by second grade. This Danish family had started the Ford dealership—tractors and model *T*s. They started a large feed company too, and then the town's propane business later in the late forties. The family had spread out with each generation, and the old house finally sold, with none of the younger families wanting to live in the big, sprawling place. Local historians had tried to rally a group to buy the house and make it into a museum, but they just couldn't make the project fly, so it had been offered for private ownership.

The house now sat on a very large lot right in the middle of residential spread—what was left of a large estate. The huge oaks and redwoods that stood guard on the property were constantly well groomed. The beautiful shady grounds were used regularly as a wedding photo venue. As I drove up the gravel drive, I compared the place with Bill and Adele's house. Brad must have really saved his pennies since high school to get into this. It had been added on to a couple of times, but the old additions had stuck close to the basic style, and it looked whole—the house looked like one continuous design.

The main block of rooms were surrounded by a wide California-bungalow type porch. There were large fist-sized, carefully trained wisteria stems crawling up the pillars and leading out onto the overhead lattice structure. The green leaves were in their glory, and the blooms just popping out. Really beautiful.

I saw Brad through the facetted glass front door, shaking hands with Del. I knocked and the door opened. Del passed me, nodded, and then went down the steps and around to the side. He must have parked in back as I hadn't seen his car.

"Come in, come in." Brad smiled wide and waved me past the doorframe and into the spacious dark front room. The absence of table lights wasn't noticeable with the flood of natural light coming in the long front windows. It was like being on the bridge of a battleship, looking out. There was polished wood crisscrossing in a craftsman-mission style ceiling and appropriate comfortable seating laid out. From the inside, the windows seemed larger. The view across the lush lawn and trees was gorgeous. Brad gestured to a plush olive-toned sofa, and I sat transfixed. I drove by the house several times a week, but it was so much more incredible from the inside.

"So, what do you think?" he gestured an arm around the interior.

"Well, I think you have a pretty terrific place. This is really beautiful, Mr. Grierson."

"Yes, it is. Didn't happen overnight, Vincent. And you can call me Brad. This is my home now after all." His gaze flowed smoothly across the front lawn and then back around to where I sat. "Can I get you something? Tea, water?"

"I'm fine, thanks." The window view made it hard to look just at him.

"I called you over to discuss something. I don't know if my brother, in his present frame of mind, would agree, but since he has been arrested, I guess I need to press ahead on my own. Do you understand that?"

"I understand what you're saying, sure."

"Vincent, we need to do some damage control for the sake of Grierson Construction. This is Adele's company too, and Ginnie's or soon will be. For their sake, we need to quiet down the kind of harmful chatter that this kind of investigation might stimulate. People won't want to buy a home from someone who smacks of criminality, to be succinct.

"I see." I saw that Brad had developed quite the piercing stare, which he now turned on. I hadn't noticed it at the luncheon.

"Any help you can give us with your recollections from that morning, any dampening down you can affect with the local constabulary would be *much* appreciated."

"I think you must have gotten the wrong impression about my influence, Brad. I don't have any special leverage with the police. And as to my story, well, I was there. I can only tell what I saw."

"I see." His eyes seemed to glimmer toward me.

"What is it you think I can do?" I held my open hands out. I was lost as to what was going on and I began to pray silently.

He smiled, and with that smile, revealed something I'm not sure I can describe adequately. There was just a hint of menace, an insinuation of deadliness that left me speechless for the moment. This was a multifaceted guy. It was as if there was another dimension going on that I didn't realize. Time seemed to slow, and it became very quiet. Suddenly I was talking to someone else, someone I didn't know *or perhaps I did*.

"I was hoping to come to a concord, Vincent. Our company will have many projects in the near future that will need sign work. It would be so much easier if we didn't have to go out to bid every time. If I knew your best interests and our best interests projected along the same lines, well, if we could *count* on your support…You have some history here in town. We're the new guys, so to speak."

All this time I had thought Brad was the fumbling older brother and Bill was the star, propping him up. This guy was a class conniver. I wondered what he really thought of me, *probably not so much*. He was obviously flattering now. I leaned forward and spread my arms wide.

"You'll have to speak a little plainer, Brad. I'm sorry, I hear you, but I don't quite get what you think I can do. I can give you fair prices, competitive prices, on any bidding I do for the projects. It sounds like you have something more specific you need first. Just what is it?"

"I was thinking about that little place on D Street where the police found the murder knife. I got the impression that you had led the police there. How did that happen?"

I told him all about striping Hilly's Impala and the neighbors seeing the convertible. "I didn't see anything, Brad. The police wouldn't let me inside, and they sure didn't share with me what they found. I didn't even know the knife was there until you just said so." I saw him wince. He knew something about it. "How did they know *it* was the knife? How did it get *there*?"

"Oh, I wouldn't worry about those details. My brother owns that house, and I'm sure he must have left it there. I believe there was some evidence of things he was planning. Maps and sketches, information that could mean trouble in the wrong hands. I thought perhaps that you—"

"But why do you think *Bill* was the one? How do *you* know?"

"It was a well-known assignation for Bill and whoever he was dallying with—well known. You know, that storybook marriage of his is on the rocks." He smiled another unpleasant smile. "Surely you weren't taken in by his sudden case of *religiosity*."

"But the neighbors saw a purple Mustang there, in the garage."

Brad winced again as I said it. He shifted in the chair, and his hand brought something up that had been buried in the cushion. The dull silver sheen of a compact AMT nine-millimeter pistol.

"I really wish you hadn't said that. I was so hoping that our association would go smoothly, Vincent." He stood and stepped over to where I sat. "Would you please stand up slowly and come with me? Oh, and your vehicle keys, please."

Hedberg house had a sizable old-fashioned basement with a sturdy stairway leading down to it through a door off the kitchen. He opened the door and down we went. Not much I could do about it. I never realized just how big nine millimeters looks from the front. It was a rain barrel pointed at me. I had a good view as Brad shoved me down into the cellar. He tied me to a floor support with scrap pieces of 12-2 Romex wire. There were other renovation supplies down here in the basement. All stored neatly. Waste not, want not. I struggled, but I wasn't getting loose soon. It hurt too much to struggle with the wire, as tight as he had made it. There was no way to fray or break the wires inside their plastic sheathing. After the door shut, under the house, it was pretty quiet, and I wondered if anyone else even knew I was here. Just Del, I guessed. It was late enough for Marti to expect me home, but there was no trail leading here. *Except for my truck in the drive.* Then I heard the truck start and move around back. Well, I guess that wasn't going to help. I heard garage doors rattle closed.

It was at least another hour before the kitchen door opened again. I saw polished loafers carefully descend to my level. My wrists were raw from struggling with the tight wire. I looked up at Brad and wondered what he planned next.

30

Supper Plans

"Are you ready for a little ride in the country, Vincent?" He unbent the long piece of electrical wire he had used to tie my waist and arms to the chair and stepped to the side quickly. He gestured with the gun, and I untied my legs from each of the chair legs with my bound hands. He gestured again, and I stood up with tingly feet. I wasn't sure I could walk without a little practice, so I fidgeted my feet to get the blood working again.

"Got a little dance for us? Why, how nice." He poked the gun in my side, and I stumbled over to the stairs. My hands were still bound together. I had to climb without much help from the handrail, so I leaned an elbow on the wall as I went up. I thought I heard a door open somewhere above, but Brad just dug the gun harder into my ribs, and I kept going. I know I was praying in heavenly tongues by the time we got up to the top step. When we got to the doorway, the gun shoved me to the left, through the kitchen. Pretty Ginnie was busy at the far counter still in her high heels. She gave me a vacant stare. A bowl was in front of her, and she was cutting up green string beans. There was the smell of something baking in the air.

"Will you be long, honey? The lasagna will be ready in half an hour." She smiled at me and looked at Brad expectantly. She was holding one of those TV knives as she spoke.

"I shouldn't be long, dear. Vincent and I just have some business to finish."

"Let's be careful as we go out the door, Vincent. No clever movements." He hissed as he kept the gun pressed in my back, and I knew it wouldn't make much noise if he fired it buried in there. I got down the porch steps to the gravel, and I heard him come crunching behind me. "Now you can just—"

"Now *you* can just put the gun down before you become very dead, my friend." Harley's voice was like a choir of angels singing "Hallelujah." I felt the gun drop away, and then the metallic crunch of it landing in the gravel. Black uniformed arms pulled me aside, and I felt the relief as the wire was twisted open at my wrists. I had to lean on the policeman to stay vertical. I don't know how he had done it, but I felt an instant surge of reprieve. Harley had found me.

The screen door slammed as two uniforms pushed inside, and I heard mixed shouting from inside the kitchen. Then the door opened again, and Ginnie stepped nonchalantly down the back stairs, her high heels firmly clipping down the steps. One of the officers had his hand on her shoulder steering her, but she stood proudly. She was escorted down the driveway and into the open door of a different unit than Brad was in. It was a circus of light as several police cars sat with their doors open and their lights flashing across the graveled yard behind the house.

Now handcuffed, Brad shouted out the cars open window, "Don't worry, honey."

He was locked in the back seat of the other unit, and Ginnie shouted out the window of her car to anyone who would listen, "My lasagna! Don't forget to turn off my lasagna!"

31

Solved by the Burrito

"**B**urritos con pollo for everybody, Luiz, and more chopped cabbage for our cheeps!" I was feeling pretty expansive. I could now walk unassisted and move my hands freely. Freedom is abstract until it's taken away. One minute you're hanging between life and death and the next you ask someone to pass the guacamole.

Harley looked like he was ready to eat the tablecloth, and Bill's expansive smile had returned now that he had been vindicated. Adele was clinging to his arm and laughing. The contractor and the detective shared some joke, probably at my expense. It was nice to see the two of them on friendly terms. Only yesterday they had been in a very different place.

"So Vincent, you got it all worked out?" Harley shoveled a chip full of salsa.

"Not so much, Detective. Like, why was Brad so upset about the purple Mustang?"

He smiled and began counting out with his fingers.

"One, the car was Ginnie's, bought for her by Clare Tribble. It's still leased to him, by the way. So it was a bread crumb. And two, Ginnie had a very short but *very* torrid affair with Clare. That was just before Brad began working with him on the building. She changed up Clare for Brad, but she kept the car."

"So that's her connection with all this?" Marti sputtered. "She's just the secretary?"

"Three, she had inherited the office building from her uncle, Calvin Marchant. No one knew. It has always been managed by a San Jose management company. She wanted to sell it to the Griersons, and being the realtor's secretary put her square in the middle of the Griersons' search for a likely building."

"*Ginnie* was SG LLC?" I almost spit my mouthful of salsa out.

"Right. Brad didn't want Bill to figure out that they were dealing off the bottom of the deck, so he had Ginnie do her incorporation in the Bay area. SG=GS, Brad switched her initials backwards on the name. His relationship with Ginnie was forged by that piece of work, I guess. That whole idea was what brought them together, like two sharks mating."

Marti leaned forward. "Well, then, is that where all the money for the Hedberg house came from?"

"That would be finger number 4."

"So Brad stabbed Clare over—"

Harley held up his thumb to stop me. "Number five. *Ginnie* stabbed Clare, not Brad." Everyone stopped their eating and talking, and there was a few seconds as the heavens re-calibrated.

"*Ginnie?* Why would Ginnie do that? She seems like such a pleasant person." Marti's voice had weakened, and I patted her arm to remind her we were in a public restaurant. I had thought that Ginnie was an airhead; it was a convincing act.

"Ginnie didn't just stab Clare, Marti. She tried to slit his throat too. She was and is a deeply angry woman. Something about her father. She just exploded that morning. Clare didn't want to let Ginnie go. He still had his eyes on her and now all her potential money too. He told her they were going to talk it out when he got back to the office, but she surprised him just before his meeting with Vincent that morning. She didn't want to share with him, it seems. I wonder what kind of deal Brad made—"

"But how did you connect the knife to Ginnie and not to Bill, or Brad? Isn't it Bill's knife that was missing?" Marti brought up the nagging problem of proof.

"That would be finger 6 or 7, I don't know. I lost count. All that cutting gave us a pretty clear forensic description of the blade profile." The detective grinned, probably to himself as much as anyone. "A knife from Bill's kitchen was in Brad's knife rack in the kitchen of the Hedberg house. Ginnie is such an obsessive housekeeper. She's more than a little anal about that. But one of *Brad's* knives was the murder weapon. We found that in the D Street house. It had been washed off, but there was still a little blood trace in the shank, under the handle. No prints of course." We all sat back to chew and think. We probably looked like cows in pasture. I'm sorry, like cows sitting around a table.

"But why would Ginnie be at the Marchant building that morning?" I asked.

"Clare didn't expect her. She just got there first. It was still her building. She wanted a last look around. She didn't know about your meeting. She's the only one who would have known, and well, you found her keys, Vincent."

"And you know that because?"

"An extra key for the Mustang was on the ring. I bet that drove her silly. She must have been looking everywhere for those keys." Everyone at the table was quiet. The key evidence had been safely forgotten in my desk drawer.

"Did she mean to stab him?" I asked after a minute.

"She brought the knife with her. The lawyers will have to work that out. You saw the huge designer bag she carried. She says that she didn't plan it. She says the knife was in her purse because she was going to return it to Adele's after she was done at the office that day. She was just looking through the building on her way to work when Clare walked in on her. He argued with her, didn't want to give her up. He should have never turned his back on her."

"So you suspected her?"

"Never considered her at all until we found the keys and the car." He shot me a quiet stare and I pinked up in embarrassment. "It is a tangled web we weave. She and he both rattled out their parts in the whole story once we separated them at the station. They're not professionals. As soon as it began to unravel, they panicked and pointed at each other. True sociopaths. They really only care about themselves."

I thought about it for a minute. "But how did you know the two sets of knives are different?" I asked.

"Finger 10, the knives have a series number stamped in the blade under the handle. The two sets had different numbers, so we could tell which went where. The lab found a very slight difference in the blade sharpening cuts too. Must have been due to subcontracting during manufacturing in China. No telling how many sets would have had the same series number with all those TV sales."

"Wow! Nineteen ninety-five, *but wait*, here's an extra set thrown in. Brad's set could have had the same series number and then we'd have never known any of this." Bill murmured, and everyone else thought over his admission.

By this time, we were all staring at the plates of steaming burritos that had been dropped in front of us. I looked around and took charge. *Somebody had to.* I grabbed hands with Marti and a startled Harley, and bowed my head. "Well, Father, *You really* pulled it off this time. Thanks for the good food and thanks for protecting us even when we didn't know we needed protecting. Amen."

We started eating, and everything was quiet for a while except for the slurping. And then Adele piped up. "Excuse me, I'm stupid or something. I get that Vinnie tipped you to the house and I get about the keys, but why did they take *my* knife in the first place? It was taken long before the murder, wasn't it?"

"That would be finger 11. I think." Harley finished chewing and swallowed. "Oldest crime in the book, my dear."

Now there's a true statement even if it sounded like W. C. Fields. It was almost a Bible quote. Out of the mouths of unbelievers.

"Ginnie was jealous of your perfect set of knives once Brad had broken one of the tips on his set. He tried to open a can of chili like they did on TV. She confided to us that she just wanted her set to be perfect again."

Perfect again, just like Eden.

"He took the replacement for her when he was at your house, under her orders. That's why she had what became the murder knife in her purse. She was embarrassed. She didn't want to throw it away, so she thought she could put it back with your set on the sly when she visited. Can I eat now? My cheese is getting cold."

As Marti and I drove home, we saw the evening pigeons floating home for the night. I thought about the doves on the porch and the pigeons in the sunset above. Flying around in their instinctual patterns, caught up in something larger. Humans are caught by our instincts too. You know, there's a bumper sticker I see frequently around town. Something about getting along: "Can't we all just get along?" Something like that? *Peace, man.* That thought is certainly an honorable one, a reasonable goal for mankind to pursue. The problem is that it is predicated on the assumption that we are all the same, and that all people are equally motivated. Constitutionally speaking, perhaps we are equal, but creatively speaking, we're not. Most people are good. But some people just choose to be bad. Such a stupid choice. God can see inside them, but we can't. That's just the way it is.

TTFN

Next time Vinnie and Marti take a long awaited vacation in Maui. Such a relaxing place…until it isn't. Surviving at the hands of international jewel thieves takes both their prayers and skills, and all this happens under the peaceful Tangerine sunset skies of Hawaii. Who'd-a-thought?

About the Author

I began my writing for my kids, coming up with stories each Christmas and scratching out adventure tales on their lunch bags. Our two kids have grown up and left the nest, so my focus has changed. After many years and ideas, I began a mystery story about a sign painter in a small town who just stumbles into volatile situations. Since I am a signpainter in a small town myself, I am well aware of the strange situations a guy can get in just doing his job. So what's the worst that can happen? How can he get out of this? That is how the "Colors" Series began, *Arterial Red* being the first of several stories.

Doing the sign thing for the past forty years has provided me with lots of material. I hope I've left out enough singular details to protect the innocent.

Experience in retail sales, school teaching, auto mechanics besides the sign world has structured my launching platform and modeled my perspectives. Applied Christianity is what I want to write about—what happens in "real" life. My Savior was gentle or bold depending on the circumstances. When do you talk about Jesus and when do you keep quiet and act like Him? When is your faith *appropriate*? Today, the news media thrive on folks who are offended by personal views and choices. Should we hold back because of it? My Heavenly Father has been careful to preserve what He says and thinks for anyone to read it in His word, the Bible. His position and judgment are secure and final. His truth is timely and significant for our lives.

CPSIA information can be obtained
at www.ICGtesting.com
Printed in the USA
FSHW010002080919
61723FS